The Adventures of an Intrepid Film Critic is journalist Anna MM Vetticad's account of a year in which she resolved to blog reviews of every single Hindi film released in the NCR (National Capital Region)...not just the high-profile, well-promoted films, or big-banner productions with major stars, but literally *every single* one of them. Through the experience of viewing and reviewing those 121 films and interviewing the people who made them, the author chronicles the changing face of Bollywood, discovering in the process an industry beyond the Vidya Balans and Priyanka Chopras, the Kapoors and the Khans. This is the other Bollywood where beautiful small films routinely disappear without a trace and where an array of dismal films are made on the sidelines to satisfy personal egos. In this book, you will meet the talented actor who trained Ranbir Kapoor for his role as a deaf-mute person in *Barfi*, but whose own debut feature flopped because of inadequate marketing. You will also meet a businessman from Mozambique who made his Bollywood debut after years of trying, a wealthy Indian industrialist laying the foundation for the acting career he is determined to have, and a former superstar lost in his own world. Through the microcosm of Bollywood, this book discusses the ethics of filmmaking, film criticism and film marketing in India, and raises important political and social questions that would concern an increasingly discerning audience.

This is a book by a sentient film reviewer whose critical tone at no point attempts to mask a deep and abiding affection for the Hindi film industry. With both humour and pathos, *The Adventures of an Intrepid Film Critic* gives readers an overview of contemporary Bollywood not attempted so far.

To

Mummy

(Susan Matthew née Koshy Chempolil)

The Adventures of an Intrepid Film Critic

Anna MM Vetticad

Foreword: Ranbir Kapoor

OM
Om Books International

Published in 2012 by

OM

Om Books International

Corporate & Editorial Office
A-12, Sector 64, Noida 201 301
Uttar Pradesh, India
Phone: +91 120 477 4100
Email: editorial@ombooks.com
Website: www.ombooksinternational.com

Sales Office
4379/4B, Prakash House, Ansari Road
Darya Ganj, New Delhi 110 002, India
Phone: +91 11 2326 3363, 2326 5303
Fax: +91 11 2327 8091
Email: sales@ombooks.com
Website: www.ombooks.com

ISBN: 978-93-81607-84-8

10 9 8 7 6 5 4 3 2 1

Printed at India

Contents

Acknowledgements

The Adventures of an Intrepid Film Critic – and everything I've done in my life so far – would not have been possible without my mother and her hotline to God on my behalf. So I'd like to say thank you to Mum and my late father who would serve as fine examples to gender-conscious, son-crazed, discriminatory parents everywhere.

Thank you Rosanna, sister, friend and my first editor on every word that I write.

Like all good Indians, especially Malayalis, I have a large extended family of siblings, cousins, uncles, aunts, nieces and nephews across the world. I'd like to thank each of them, especially my immediate family, for their encouragement and advice. But most of all, I'd like to thank my brother Thomas who seems to believe in me even more than I believe in myself. Thank you too to my 'awesome' nephew Matthew, budding editorial consultant and all-round 'dude'.

My friend Jaya Bhattacharji Rose, a big hug for all the guidance and that perennial shoulder to cry on.

Ajay Mago of Om Books International, thank you for taking pride in your authors. My editor Dipa Chaudhuri, thank you for your affection for my manuscript, and for helping me crystallise my thoughts.

My fellow critics Arnab Banerjee, Namrata Joshi, Shubhra Gupta and Suparna Sharma, thank you for the support and friendship, and for forgiving me my long absence from our *adda*s because of this book. Thank you Madhusudan Srinivas, the ever-resourceful and helpful Gautam Chintamani, and young Mihir Pandya who really must stop calling me Ma'am – those *adda*s are never the same without you. Thank you Bandeep Singh – you may not remember this, but you were the one who urged me to 'look beyond' that office desk.

Thank you Maneesha Dube for mentoring me without quite knowing it, Rohit Brijnath for being the best boss I've ever had, and my friend Amrith Lal for redefining feminism for me.

An additional thank you to Jaya, Suparna and Maneesha for your invaluable feedback on my manuscript.

Ranbir Kapoor, thank you for everything.

My lawyer Christine Chiramel, thank you for demystifying the intimidating maze of legalese.

All the wonderful people I've got to know through the online social media, I'm so grateful for your generosity and feedback. I had not met New York-based journalist Aseem Chhabra even once when he took the trouble to tweet me, suggesting that I turn my blog *annavetticadgoes2themovies* into a book, long before I had shared my plans with friends. 'A big shout out' too – as they say in Twitter-ese – to my virtual buddies Ram P Singh of Seattle, Mallika Gupta of Chandigarh, Moses

Sapir of Tirat Carmel in Haifa, Israel, Rana Safvi of Dubai, Aniruddha Chatterjee of Kolkata, Shekhar Iyer of Delhi and so many others for the goodwill and the constant interest in my work that I find so reassuring. Whaddyaknow Aniruddha, I tracked down Vipinno!

Thank you Dr LK Malhotra, Ginni Chadha, Jackie Shroff, Jayaditya Gupta, Jyotika Ahuja, Natasha Pal, Punit Sahaya, Rajnigandha Shekhawat, Renuka Narayanan, Rohini Bhandari, Rohini Iyer, Sam M Elangalloor, Sabah Kazi, Saurav Sen, Shamir Tandon, Varnika Gupta and Vidyottama P Sharma for helping me with my research. Thank you Kamal Jain, Sanjeev Lamba and Siddharth Roy Kapur for your patience and time. Thank you Shanti Malik for being so understanding. Rauf Ahmed, thank you for being ever willing to share your experiences with a younger colleague.

Your Excellency Bishop Ignatius Loyola Mascarenhas, thank you for the many kindnesses and prayers when we've needed them most. Thank you Neville Lobo, Liam Deasy and Kevin Ward for everything I've learnt from you.

A very special word for my English teacher Deepa Sarobar of the Convent of Jesus and Mary School, New Delhi. Ma'am, you and my parents are the ones who first taught me to love language and literature, so thank you!

Thank you to every brick and wall, every nook and cranny, every teacher and student of Jesus and Mary College, Delhi University, for being a part of such an important turning point in my life. Thank you Susan Mehrotra and Meera Kaul for the lasting friendship.

Finally, a salute to every member of the film industry who has the courage and the honesty to admit – not just in private, but on public platforms too – that they do care about reviews, especially those written by critics they respect. And to their colleagues who say, 'to hell with reviews'...you fuel my passion for film criticism more than you can imagine, so most of all, I thank you!

Foreword

When Anna first told me about this project, I was intrigued. The account of a year spent reviewing every single Hindi film released in the National Capital Region that would provide us with an overview of the industry...sounded like an ambitious and back-breaking exercise to me! But here we are now. *The Adventures of an Intrepid Film Critic* is complete and I believe it will be a significant addition to the sparse library of literature available on the Hindi film industry.

For the past decade, there has been a steady increase in the number of books being written about specific Hindi films and stars. As readers lap up such works, publishers have begun to sense the potential of this market and have been commissioning more such ventures. The genre most commonly being explored in this area is the biography, as I'm sure you have noticed. Fortunately or unfortunately for us actors, large sections of the public seem to be fascinated by the lives we lead, and are keen to know as much as they possibly can about us. It goes without saying that if so many reams of newsprint are devoted to our personal stories, then exhaustive memoirs would be popular too. Similarly, if a particular film has been a hit or has achieved the status of a classic, then it's evident that people would be keen on a detailed analysis of that film.

What's been more or less missing from our bookstores though is a look at the bigger picture, an evaluation of the history of Hindi cinema and an examination of the present state of the film industry. That's where *The Adventures of an Intrepid Film Critic* comes in, providing material with both humour and depth to the general public and especially to students of cinema in India and abroad.

I myself have gathered many interesting insights from my discussions with Anna about this book. As a member of the film industry, I have never hesitated to admit that I come from a position of privilege. Being the great grandson of the legendary Prithviraj Kapoor, the grandson of Raj Kapoor, the grand nephew of Shammi and Shashi Kapoor, the son of Rishi and Neetu Kapoor, it's obvious that opportunities have come my way that would not be easily available to outsiders trying to make it in this industry. But the other side of the coin is that not every person from a film family necessarily succeeds in films. Lineage can get you a foot in the door, but it's entirely up to you to walk the right path and build a meaningful career for yourself.

Whether you are from a film family or an outsider, what primarily distinguishes a successful star from others who had similar opportunities are the choices we make – our choice of scripts, choice of co-stars, choice of directors and production houses to work with. I'm no longer a newcomer but as a young actor still finding my way around the profession, I am particularly interested in the section in this book about strugglers in the industry – including former beauty contest winners and prominent models – who are taking up projects that they admit they are not proud of. I've never been in their position, but I do belong to a generation that has grown up watching, admiring and loving an actor who is one of the biggest stars our country has ever seen, although he came in with no film connections whatsoever – Mr Shah Rukh Khan. The lesson I've learnt from following his career is that if we have faith in ourselves and the means to bide our time, then that's what we ought to do: do our best, be patient and wait till a worthwhile film comes our way instead of settling for less or, even worse, what some people describe as 'C-grade ventures'.

Incidentally, I've always been aware of the existence of such films somewhere at the back of my mind. They appear and disappear from our newspaper listings. No one I know seems to watch them, and yet they are made on a regular basis. So far I've not got down to inquiring further about them but I'm quite fascinated by the stories Anna tells about these films that seem to be made in a different realm of the industry altogether.

It's unfortunate that so much money is wasted on such films while some lovely small productions struggle for marketing budgets to attract audiences. Hopefully, in the coming years our industry will figure out ways of promoting good quality, low-cost ventures more effectively. For this, we will of course need the cooperation of the Indian media that, for the moment, is too focused on big films with big stars.

I'm thrilled that Anna has devoted so much space to small films in her book. Most of you have probably not heard of *Shor in the City*, yet my friend and *Rockstar* director Imtiaz Ali tells me that it was, in his opinion, perhaps THE film of 2011. I'm told that director Onir's *I Am* is a very brave film, but it too has not been seen by enough people. No doubt marketing such films is a challenge but I'd like to believe it's not an impossible task. Mr Salman Khan's support for *Chillar Party* brought the spotlight on this children's film that may otherwise have struggled for an audience. In my own little way, by doing the 'item number' 'Tai tai phiss' for *Chillar Party,* I was trying to push a film that I felt deserved to be seen by many people.

I must confess, however, that the film I'm happiest to see being discussed in this book is another one with which I have a distant connection. *Bubble Gum* stars an ensemble cast of gifted youngsters including Sohail Lakhani who trained me for my role as a deaf-mute person in *Barfi*. Sohail, who is deaf in real life, played a deaf-mute teenager in *Bubble Gum,* his first film. He helped me with my body language and sign language for my film. During the time we spent together, I was amazed at his positive attitude despite the odds that he battles every day. His optimism made me rather ashamed of the occasions when I've grumbled about the comparatively minor problems in my life. As it happens, he is talented and a good teacher.

Sohail wants acting to be his profession. For his sake then, I'm glad to note that *Bubble Gum* is discussed in this book not for philanthropic reasons but because it's a quality product featuring quality actors like him and all his co-stars. My best wishes will always be with Sohail. I look forward to meeting him as a colleague in the field.

There are several others like him that this book will introduce you to – actors who have not yet become household names either because they're acting in the wrong films or because their films have not received the marketing backing they deserve. As our industry evolves, we will probably see changes on this front in the coming years. Our big films are getting bigger by the day, cornering more screens in theatres, with promotions on a scale never seen before, as Anna notes in this book. What we need now is to find a way for big and small films to co-exist.

I'd like to congratulate Anna for her book. The title is apt. Only 'an intrepid film critic' could have provided us with the insights that you will find here as she persisted with her year-long mission to watch films that the rest of us either never hear of or deliberately stay away from.

For the sake of every film buff out there, I hope that this is the first of many books Anna writes on the industry.

Ranbir Kapoor

Author's Note

My goal in writing this book is to provide film buffs and students of cinema with an overview of the Hindi film industry as it is today. This is not an academic treatise though. My aim is to put my point across with a light touch that would make this book accessible to people who love films but don't necessarily get to spend as much time wandering the corridors of Bollywood as I do.

Before I begin though, it's important to have some clarity on my use of the term 'Bollywood'. For me personally, the word is now a matter of convenience more than anything else. 'Bollywood' in this book signifies the film industry that is based in Mumbai and makes primarily Hindi films. I say 'primarily Hindi' in the context of a changing scenario from which has emerged Abhinay Deo's *Delhi Belly*, Kiran Rao's *Dhobi Ghat* and Rohit Shetty's *Singham* in 2011. *Delhi Belly* is a mostly English film that was additionally dubbed in Hindi. *Dhobi Ghat* used English and Hindi in equal measure. *Singham* was in Hindi with a generous infusion of Marathi dialogues and one entire sequence in Tulu. All three came from the same industry that has given us the Hindi-Punjabi *Vicky Donor* in 2012 while out-and-out Hindi cinema remains its mainstay.

It's with this definition in mind that I have not included in this book a film like *Breakaway* also known as *Speedy Singhs* although it was released in 2011 which is this book's catchment year. Not because this film is in English, but because it did not come from the Mumbai film industry. To my mind, *Speedy Singhs* would not fall under the larger umbrella term 'Indian cinema' either, although it was co-produced by Bollywood star Akshay Kumar, featured him in a guest appearance, was about the Indian Sikh community in Canada, and starred several Indian actors and Canadian actors of Indian origin. Keep in mind though that it's a Canadian story in a Canadian setting with a Canadian co-producer, and those actors of Indian origin were mostly Canadian. That makes *Speedy Singhs* a Canadian-Indian venture. Then again, to call it Bollywood or even Indian cinema is less far-fetched than claiming ownership of that iconic 2008 film *Slumdog Millionaire*. Sure, *Slumdog* had an Indian story set in Mumbai, was based on a book by an Indian writer, featured an almost entirely Indian cast and a sizeable percentage of the film's crew was Indian. However, it was directed by a Briton, produced by a Briton and distributed by UK and US companies. Going by accepted norms, it's a British film while also being that rare example of a truly international collaboration.

That brings me back to my use of the term 'Bollywood' in this book. I've gone into this explanation because films like director Onir's *I Am* have their origins in the Mumbai film industry but are far removed from what is traditionally perceived as Bollywood fare. Some film commentators may disagree with me but I don't choose to define Bollywood only as a source of mass-appealing, larger-than-life, colourful cinema featuring song and dance, to be contrasted with the more offbeat films that also emerge from the Mumbai film industry. I believe films such as Onir's *I Am* (2011) and Vikramaditya Motwane's *Udaan* (2010) are as much Bollywood as films on the scale of, say, Farhan Akhtar's *Don* (2006) and Anees Bazmee's *Ready* (2011).

Having said that, I realise that there are a few members of the Mumbai film industry who take offence at the term. To them I'm tempted to say, I'll stop using the word 'Bollywood' when Bollywood stops lifting stories, concepts and entire films from Hollywood, the rest of the world and even the rest of India without legitimately purchasing rights or acknowledging sources. However, that would be impetuous on my part, and would completely mislead you about my intentions, since neither is the *entire* industry guilty of this crime nor do I use Bollywood as a pejorative term. It just happens to be an expedient, practical word that signifies the crazy heterogeneous mix of films big and small made in Mumbai that – like millions of people worldwide – I happen to love very much.

1

Let the Masochism Begin!

This is a book on masochism. No seriously, I'm not being flippant. This is a book about self-inflicted pain and the pleasure derived thereof. There's an expression in Hindi for it: *'Apne hi paao pe kulhaadi maarna'* (to axe one's own foot). That's what this is: an axe that I picked up on January 1 last year and smashed right into my own foot, month after month after month!

It all began with a strange New Year resolution – to blog reviews of every Bollywood film released in my home city Delhi and its suburbs without missing a single one as far as possible. Most of us are aware that India is the world's largest producer of films, but the point was well and truly driven home to me only when I embarked upon this little adventure. I drove long distances to visit theatres I had not set eyes on before, to see films that were not being released anywhere else in Delhi. I discovered areas in the National Capital Region that I have not seen before in the city of my birth where I have spent all my life. I took just one 10-day vacation from viewing and reviewing in these 365 days, but returned home to a backlog of nearly a dozen films – yes, THAT'S how many Hindi films are released! I contacted producers to procure unreleased DVDs of films I missed while on that brief break. And by the end of the year, I had 121 reviews on my blog *annavetticadgoes2themovies*, of films showing within a 60-70 km radius of my home – there were about half a dozen that were beyond the reach of even my determination and dedication.

It was a physically exhausting, financially consuming, intellectually draining exercise! Imagine then what I would have endured if I'd decided to cover every film made in every Indian language, not just Hindi! I would have gone bankrupt and passed out from fatigue, I guess.

You may well ask what I gained from this bizarre undertaking! Well for a start, I thought I knew until now how bad a truly bad film can be, but I learnt that it can actually get worse. The public may rant against *Ram Gopal Varma ki Aag*, Mani Ratnam's *Raavan* and Anurag Basu's *Kites*, but let me assure you that these were bad films which still maintained certain basic standards that we as viewers have a right to take for granted. As a film journalist though, I've had the misfortune of watching some films so terrible and so beyond debate that I wonder why anyone bothered to make them! My worst experience in the pre-2011 era of my life had been an icky film called *Ladies Tailor* in which the leading man (Rajpal Yadav) gets turned on while measuring his female customers' thighs, and *Deshdrohi* starring Kamaal Rashid Khan a.k.a. KRK who needs training in walking, talking, standing, sitting, smiling and even staring into space.

And then in 2011, when I watched *Tension Doooor* (yes, with four 'o's which I will explain later in this book), *Be-Careful*, *Chitkabrey – Shades of Grey*, *Tum Hi To Ho* and *Ye Stupid Pyar*, I realised that there exists a parallel universe of pathetic films that most viewers are not even aware of – films made by indulgent parents to satisfy the vanity of their misguided sons; films in which rich businessmen cast themselves in moments of self-indulgent weakness; films sometimes made by people who genuinely don't realise they are not cut out for this field; films by delusional filmmakers who blame their box-office failures on audience indifference to niche cinema, not on the indifferent quality of their work; films made by once-respected people (it hurts me to say this) who stubbornly refuse to hang up their boots.

In this parallel universe, well-established names sometimes agree to be associated with sub-standard products. Perhaps they assume that no one will watch the film, and the stain on their curriculum vitae will go unnoticed. Perhaps they are beyond caring. Perhaps the film sounded good at the concept stage. Perhaps it was a personal favour. Or perhaps they are close to someone associated with the project. Did you know that the legendary and now-nearly-retired Lata Mangeshkar sang for a dismal children's film titled *Satrangee Parachute* in 2011?! Well she did. The song in question was composed by Shamir Tandon, best known for 'Kitne ajeeb rishtey hai yahaan pe' in Mangeshkar's voice from Madhur Bhandarkar's National Award-winning film *Page 3*! *Satrangee Parachute* also featured the voices of Rahat Fateh Ali Khan, Shaan, Kailash Kher, Usha

Uthup and Shreya Ghosal! Famous voices, however, could do little to redeem this film in which the child hero pees into a bottle because the toilet is occupied and his urine is sold by mistake to a policeman who screams at the seller: '*Gareeb hoke pishaab pila raha hai to tu ameer banke kya latrine ka dosa khilayega?*' (If, being a poor man, you are serving me pee, when you get rich will you serve me a *dosa* made of shit?) That dialogue marked the pinnacle of humour in the film!

Debutant director Vineet Khetrapal tells me he signed up Tandon to get access to Mangeshkar. Tandon – who shares the music direction credits for *Satrangee Parachute* with Kaushik Dutta – explains Mangeshkar's involvement in the film: 'It's just my relationship with Lataji that got her to sing the song. She has a certain musical fondness for the tunes I create and I'm extremely fortunate that the last four songs she's done have been for me.'

He willingly describes for me the many alternative processes involved in music direction in Bollywood. Though it may seem like the natural thing to do, Hindi filmmakers don't always share their scripts or even storylines with music directors. Sometimes they simply buy off tunes from the composer's existing bank; sometimes they ask for the customisation of an already created melody to suit a particular context; sometimes they simply come looking for any up-tempo, raunchy number that would serve as an 'item' song. And then of course there are the more well-rounded collaborations of the sort that Tandon has had with Bhandarkar, where the music director reads the script, understands the situations and composes specifically for the film. As for the impact of a dud like *Satrangee Parachute* on his standing, Tandon says: 'We as music directors give our songs to filmmakers hoping that they are in safe hands, that they will be picturised well, that the film will be successful and we'll all take pride in being associated with the project. But we don't have control over the kind of film being made. That's why we try to work with like-minded people. Even then, you can't always tell because sometimes there might be a newcomer with a great spark who might make a good film.'

Be that as it may, it broke my heart a little when I saw Shankar Mahadevan – one of contemporary India's finest singers – lend not just his voice but his face as well to a tacky film called *Masti Express* in which he actually made a guest appearance! And if Kunal Ganjawala – he of the voice with the bell-like clarity – can prove that he did not once feel the urge to giggle while singing 'Turban victory' in that overbearingly loud, divisive film called *I Am Singh,* I will eat my shoes, my hat and this book with it! Read this and you will know what I mean:

Bole so nihaal
Sat shri akaal
We live for the turban
We die for the turban
It's all about the turban
Victory!
With all our might, we'll fight for justice
We'll fight for the right
With all our might, we'll fight for justice
We'll fight for the right
We are the warriors
Our turban is our pride

Our turban's our pride
Yeah, we are the warriors
Our turban is our pride
Our turban's our pride
... Oho, oh oh, oh yeah yeah yeah ee yeah...
Don't preach the hate
Don't spread the rut
We'll give it back
We'll make you shut
And if you call us any names
You'll regret, and feel the shame...

Take a moment, dear reader, to recover from that.

Now swallow this: Ganjawala was accompanied on 'Turban victory' by none other than Sukhwinder Singh, winner of multiple awards in India and abroad, the voice of Shah Rukh Khan in a number of smash hits ranging from 'Chhaiyya chhaiyya' to 'Chak de India', and known internationally for 'Jai Ho' from *Slumdog Millionaire*! Earlier in the year, I'd seen Sukhwinder make an appearance and sing a closing track to accompany the end credits in a film called *Angel* marked not just by its mediocre production values, but by its insensitive treatment of a character with a disability. The reputation of these singers remains intact in spite of 'Turban victory', because the millions who've heard and loved Sukhwinder's 'Jai Ho' or Ganjawala's 'Bheege hotth tere' and their numerous other super-successes, have no idea of the existence of this embarrassing excuse for a song.

In the space inhabited by films like *I Am Singh*, a space alien to regular Hindi film viewers, you will find once-big stars who simply went off the radar past their prime. They make a living here or do favours to friends and former colleagues by acting in their films, alongside character artistes whose life-long struggles are camouflaged by the pancake on tinseltown's glamorous façade. Ayesha Jhulka was Aamir Khan's leading lady in 1992's *Jo Jeeta Wohi Sikandar*. Nearly 20 years later, there she was dancing wildly as a guest at a couple of parties in an oddity of a film called *Na Jaane Kabse*. I'm not kidding, that's all she did in the film – appeared in passing in a crowd, danced, disappeared, appeared fleetingly once again in another song, danced, disappeared. I learnt later from director Pammi Somal that Ayesha initially had a larger role in the script but her character was scissored out for various reasons, by which time those two songs had already been shot. When Nirmal Pandey starred as Vikram Mallah Mastana in Shekhar Kapur's internationally applauded hit *Bandit Queen* in 1994, he was hailed as an actor to watch out for. Despite a handful of acclaimed performances in niche films, his career graph did not live up to those early expectations. Years after he played Phoolan Devi's charismatic lover, I remember catching a glimpse of him in a few-seconds-long, non-speaking guest appearance in producer-actor Kamaal R Khan's obnoxiously acrimonious *Deshdrohi* in 2008 for which Khan tells me he paid the actor just ₹ 20,000. In 2011, less than a year after his passing away, came what must have been his last big-screen appearance – in an obscure film called *Vikalp* in which he hammed his way through the role of an Indian policeman in Bangkok. *Vikalp* was so poorly received that I had to visit Satyam cineplex in Delhi's Nehru Place two days in a row to convince the manager to run it – the film was in newspaper listings, but he explained that it's financially unviable for the theatre to hold a show if only one ticket has been sold!

And then there's former superstar Jackie Shroff... If you tend to watch only high-profile films, you would not know what I now do – that Shroff has not retired from Bollywood. He acted in five Hindi films that were released in 2011. They ranged from substantial supporting roles in godawful films to ill-conceived guest appearances. That they came in a year when he received critical acclaim as the lead in the National Award-winning Tamil film *Aaranya Kaandam* simply aggravated my heartbreak over his forgotten presence in Bollywood.

My story is not just about old-timers though. As a journalist, I've known for years how unimaginably difficult it is for an aspiring actor to get a foot in the door in this cruel industry. But these 365 days of agony and ecstasy taught me that it's even worse than I had assumed it is.

Rajniesh Duggall is one of India's most prominent models, the Grasim Mr India 2003 winner and Mr International 2003 1st runner-up. Have quality film offers not been flowing in for this handsome man? As I watched him in *Be-Careful* in 2011, I could think of no other explanation for why he would act in a raucous, cringe-inducing film about two Indian sex maniacs who go to Bangkok to get away from their wives and get laid.

Back in 2009, I was in France to report on the Cannes Film Festival when I met Miss India World 2008 Parvathy Omanakuttan. There she was, a tall and striking girl floating around, introducing herself to guests at a party hosted by Vijay Mallya at a castle on the French Riviera. I was one of the few

TICKETS

journalists present and I'm sure my colleague's bulky camera bag made us pretty noticeable. Whatever be the reason, Ms Omanakuttan stopped to say hello. You cannot believe how difficult it is to gain an entry into Bollywood, she told me and, no, you're wrong, *Femina* no longer promotes their Miss India winners as they used to. Two years later, alone in a hall in Delhi's Vasant Kunj with only ushers for company, my guffaws were laced with sympathy as I watched that attractive former beauty queen's debut Hindi film *United Six*.

Director Vishal Aryan Singh's film starring Parvathy tells us the story of six Indian girls in Bangkok who are tired of the struggles life throws their way. So they decide to rob a bank. The plot they hatch is too puerile to bear repeating here. *United Six* is one of those films that's so bad, it's good. The poor production quality, terrible terrible bit part players, shoddy writing and tawdry dialogues are all unintentionally funny. Unconvinced by the bank robbery plan, one of the girls says in true Hindi *filmi* style: '*Itna aasaan thodi na hai. Yeh izzat thodi na hai jo loot li.*' (C'mon, robbing a bank is not as simple as robbing a person of their honour.) And when the rest of her friends keep referring to a horny policeman as 'KLPD', the duh among them asks if they mean 'Kuala Lumpur Police Department'. I'd say that line was worth the price of my ticket!

Seriously though, was it desperation that drove Parvathy to sign up for such a non-starter?! Well, one of the nice things about being a journalist is that when I have such questions on my mind, the answer is often just a phone call away. So, I dial Parvathy. 'The kind of roles I was getting after the Miss India win were the sort that required me to wear a swimsuit, and it really didn't matter whether the girl is in the film or not,' she tells me. 'The wait to break the mould was kind of getting to me. That's when I heard the script of *United Six* and I really liked it because when the director narrated it to me, I could see every scene before my eyes. Though I had my doubts, because it was a film with five other girls, all of them newcomers, and this was the production house's first film too. Yet I told myself, you've waited almost two years and nothing has come your way, so why not utilise this opportunity? At least it will be an experience.'

Parvathy admits that she is not proud of *United Six*. The lesson in this for her has been that there's a difference between a good narration and the actual film 'when production values, the quality of the film used, the promotions, etc. make a big difference'. She concedes too that it's tougher now to get another Hindi film offer because people tend to have reservations about an actress whose first film didn't work out. But she insists she has no regrets because 'the experience enriched me as a person' and it taught her 'to be patient'.

I don't know whether newcomers like Rajniesh Duggall and Parvathy Omanakuttan are in a position to walk out midway through a project when they realise it has the potential to be damaging. I do wonder though whether it's a mistake not to do so in a profession where brand value counts for so much.

I go in search of an answer from a star who has been through the grind, who has made it big in the industry without any film family connections. Vidya Balan is busy promoting *Kahaani* when I accost her with the query: What would you say if these youngsters were to come to you for advice? Vidya replies with a conviction that has clearly stood her in good stead: 'If you know it's a production that you will not enjoy then you shouldn't do it. What kind of experience will you get from a cringe-worthy production or performance or character? ... You have to have the patience and have the faith in yourself to be able to hold it out. I do realise that people come from all parts of the country to this industry, and often they have to compromise because it's a matter of survival. But if it isn't that, and you can wait it out, you should. Even if you have to take up other jobs while you wait for the right opportunity as an actor, it's fine. But do what you believe in...' (Full interview: p. 180)

Life isn't as bad for Rajniesh and Parvathy as it is for many others. Rajniesh has, after all, already played the lead for producer/director Vikram Bhatt in three films that he can list on his bio-data without wincing at the mention of their names: *1920* with which he made his debut, *Phhir* which was released in 2011 and the 3D film *Dangerous Ishhq* in 2012 which marked Karisma Kapoor's comeback in Bollywood. As this book goes to press, Parvathy has made a start in south India with her debut Tamil film *Billa 2* (the sequel to the Ajith-starrer *Billa* which was a remake of SRK's *Don* and Rajinikanth's old superhit *Billa* both of which in turn were remakes of the 1978 Amitabh Bachchan-starrer *Don*). Hopefully then their stories will have a happy ending. My book certainly does.

Lost in the melee of sub-par films some of which are heavily promoted and some not, I found sweet surprises like *I Am*, *Bubble Gum* and the non-Bollywood, primarily English film *Memories in March*. It's the discovery of such films that reinforces my conviction that in the life of a critic, every film deserves a chance. This does not mean that a critic *has to* see every film ever made – that's not humanly possible! What it means is that we should not pre-judge films. In the past when I've cribbed to colleagues about the trauma of watching bad films, I've often been asked, 'So who's forcing you to watch them? Why don't you just watch the good ones?' I've always responded with, 'How would I know in advance whether a film is good or bad?' Oddly enough, this rather obvious question flummoxes most people. But you'd be surprised at the number of times I've been told by non-film journalists that they thought 'any film journalist with experience' would have developed an 'instinct' over the years that would help them guess. Really? Guess?

On further discussion, I've discovered that what they really mean is that film journalists and critics should skip small films and only bother with big banner ventures. Well, considering the tosh and twaddle that some prominent names have subjected us to in the past, how fair would that be? Besides, if critics were to watch only hyped-up, highly-visible films, all the three that I just cited would have been ignored. If those so-called 'instincts' were inspired by track records, then of the three, the only one I might have watched would be director Onir's *I Am* since he earlier made *My Brother Nikhil*, a moving portrayal of the life of India's first officially recorded HIV/AIDS patient starring Sanjay Suri, Juhi Chawla and Purab Kohli. I knew nothing about Sanjivan Lal and Sanjoy Nag but if that had become an excuse to skip their 2011 films, the loss would have been mine. Lal's *Bubble Gum* is an unusually sensitive Hindi film about sibling rivalry in a household where one child has a speech and hearing impairment. And Nag's *Memories in March* is a gutsy rarity in a country that would rather pretend that homosexuality does not exist. Sadly though, all three floundered without an audience because of their poor or zero marketing budgets and/or strategies.

What you're about to read then, are my experiences and all that I learnt about the Mumbai film industry during a year spent reviewing *every single Bollywood film released in the National Capital Region of India* on my personal blog. Not just the high-profile well-promoted films, not just those considered 'significant' by the media or sections of the public, but literally every single Bollywood film – known or unknown, big, small or tiny! The experience – quite unexpectedly – has left me with a 360 degree overview of Bollywood, even more passion for this industry than I had when I began and more patience than I thought was possible.

Okay, enough of rumination now! Let the masochism begin!

2

Dr Vivek Sudershan PhD

It's a cold January day in Delhi. I'm at the press preview of a dubious film called *Impatient Vivek* starring an attractive former Miss India runner-up Sayali Bhagat and a scientist-cum-businessman-cum-aspiring-actor from Ghaziabad called Vivek Sudershan.

A heroine who is not attracted to the hero yet does not seem to mind his devotion, a hero who kidnaps the girl on the assumption that his persistent pursuit of her will ultimately bear fruit ... with these ingredients, *Impatient Vivek* follows in the footsteps of numerous Hindi films that have encouraged roadside Romeos in their belief that the way to a woman's heart is through sexual harassment. But unlike many of its predecessors, this film does not boast of a well-known cast to divert attention from its irresponsible storyline. The jokes about rape and masturbation only make it worse. The central character Vivek is nicknamed IV by friends and family – because his father thinks he's Idiot Vivek, mom thinks he's

Incredible Vivek, he considers himself Impatient Vivek, but his lady love concludes that he's actually Innocent Vivek! No doubt this was considered a clever bit of scripting by the film maker since he chose to reveal the full form of IV right at the end. He forgot to add another option: Insufferable Vivek!

The actor playing IV is a telling specimen from the shadowy world on the outskirts of Bollywood. Have money, will act. If the late Gulshan Kumar could thrust his brother Kishen on the nation with the conviction that marketing alone can create a star, why should Vivek Sudershan be deterred by his lack of acting talent and screen presence? *Impatient Vivek* is produced by Sudershan's company Search Film's (sic) Production, directed and scripted by his filmmaker friend Rahat Kazmi, and based on a story by BK Tyagi, a scientist in Vigyan Prasar, an autonomous body that comes under the Central government's Department of Science and Technology.

I've not seen the director's earlier film *Dekh Re Dekh*, but a gaggle of Hindi journalists outside the preview theatre tell me I should not judge him by the abysmal quality of *Impatient Vivek*. Okay, so I'll be fair. A few months later, as I settle down to write this book, I dial his number. 'You want to talk to me about *Impatient Vivek*?!' Kazmi's soft voice sounds incredulous at the other end of the line. I explain the concept of my book to him, and he in turn is at pains to explain that he believes in meaningful cinema. 'I regret having done this film. But sometimes when you are part of a group, you can't take a decision. Vivek is a good friend. It's not like he pushed me to do this film. It might even have worked with a big star, but it was a wrong choice for Vivekji because it's so different from what he is. He's 32, a common-looking guy, not very polite, rustic... I told him, "You don't look like a hero, it's better that we do something simple with you." Instead we gave him a chocolatey boy role in a romcom.'

I'm not sure I'd use the label 'chocolatey boy' for a hero who walks up to his leading lady and asks her more than once, 'Can I rape you?' in scenes that are clearly intended to be comical! I'm not sure I'd ascribe the romantic comedy genre to a crass film in which the leading man interrupts impending coitus with a foreigner picked up from a Goan beach, inexplicably rushes from the bed to the bathroom and begins pumping air into a basketball while the camera rests on his hunched and heaving back, in an obvious effort to convince us that he's masturbating! The memory of it makes me shiver with revulsion, but Kazmi sounds so sweet and humble that I almost feel guilty about asking tough questions. So I venture to inquire as mildly as possible whether the 'joke' about rape was an error of judgement. And there it comes...the answer just pours out of him, his bitterness and resentment simmering beneath that gentle tone...

'Can I tell you something frankly?' he asks. Sure, go ahead. 'Aamir Khan makes a film, I'm forgetting the title... *Delhi Belly*...and there are certain extremely extremely vulgar dialogues like when that guy [Vir Das] comes to the girl's wedding. What he's thinking and what he says are so vulgar that I can't say them out to you just now, but critics are writing in their reviews that "full respect to Aamir Khan". So what was the difference in using the word "rape" in my film? "Rape" has been used thousands of times in Hindi films. Even in *Mann* he says, "*Isne toh maansik balaatkaar kar diya.*" (He has commited mental rape.) *Balaatkaar* and rape, what difference is there? Openly you are saying. But because we are not a big banner and all that, we took "A" certificate but still people take it with a different point of view. Rape is a very common word that everybody can use. Also from the title you can see that the guy Vivek is an impatient guy, a stupid guy, and if he's drunk, he can speak any stupid things.'

Comparing *Impatient Vivek* and *Delhi Belly*? Hmmm… That's the entire point of finesse, Mr Kazmi. You can have a crude character in a film, but it's the director and script's handling of the character that determines whether the film as a whole is crude. That's why a love-making scene shot by two vastly different filmmakers can turn out so different, one distasteful and the other aesthetic.

And while on the subject of rape, I do wish Hindi filmmakers – from A to Z grade – would appreciate that there's nothing humorous about the violation of one human being by another. Maybe these people who find rape so amusing should be forced to volunteer at hospital emergency rooms and rape crisis centres to see up close the impact of this base crime.

Kazmi is not the only inhabitant of low-brow filmdom whose repertoire of gags covers sexual violence. Remember I told you about *Be-Careful* starring model Rajniesh Duggall? In a scene from that film, comedian Sanjay Mishra (a talented man who really should know better) walks up to a woman and asks if he can rape her. When her boyfriend (Rajpal Yadav) lands up and demands to know what happened, Mishra nonchalantly replies: '*Arrey, sister ko bol raha hoon, chalo, rape karke do minute mein drop kar denge. Maan nahin rahi hai.*' (I told this lady that I'll rape her and drop her back here in two minutes, but she just doesn't agree.) If you don't believe me, please visit YouTube and watch the film's promotional trailer.

When I bring up this scene with Duggall in a conversation shortly afterwards, he is embarrassed. 'I told the director not to include such things in the film,' he says regretfully. '*Be-Careful* was a big mistake for me. The narration made it sound like it would be a good slapstick comedy. I was also given a different picture about who the rest of the cast would be, including the guy who would play the joint leading man with me. I was told it would be someone like Kunal Khemu [from Madhur Bhandarkar's *Traffic Signal* and Rohit Shetty's *Golmaal 3*] or Muzammil Ibrahim [a fellow A-list model]. But the person who ultimately played the role was partly financing the film, and while we were shooting, I realised that this was definitely not the sort of project I should have been in.'

Films like *Be-Careful* play to the gallery with their coarse sexism because certain sections of the male audience enjoy watching women being ravaged, insulted and debased. You don't have to dredge the bottom of the barrel to know this though. Just watch Anees Bazmee's 2011 film *Thank You* starring Akshay Kumar, Sonam Kapoor, Irrfan Khan, Rimi Sen, Bobby Deol, Suneil Shetty and Celina Jaitley. Listening to the not-so-gentle men in the hall whistle, hoot, clap and cheer with glee each time Irrfan's character insulted his wife, I realised why my friend Gautam had warned me against watching morning shows alone at MGF Metropolitan Mall in Gurgaon.

At a much much tamer level, there was a scene in Imtiaz Ali's *Jab We Met* in 2007 that bothered me greatly, coming as it did in the middle of a film I admire so much. Geet (Kareena Kapoor) keeps goading Aditya (Shahid Kapoor) about the possibility that he might rape her if they share a hotel room, and he assures Geet that he will do no such thing. It's meant to be an amusing exchange, I suspect. Aditya repeats the 'joke' later in the film. Girls, there's got to be a better way of telling a boy that you are apprehensive about being alone with him. Boys, there's got to be a better way of telling a girl that she's safe in your company. *Et tu*, Imtiaz?

Whew! I really needed to let off that steam!

So as you may have figured, *Impatient Vivek* does not bode well for the rest of my year. For the record, I sent numerous messages to the film's hero Vivek Sudershan through his director, wrote to him on Facebook, emailed and phoned his office. When he finally responded with a mail, it was to excuse himself from an interview.

Dr BK Tyagi – the scientist on whose story *Impatient Vivek* is based – considers the film so bad that he even requested me not to write about it. In an agitated e-mail sent late one night he wrote: 'Unfortunately, Rahat (director Rahat Kazmi) has totally failed in capturing the true soul and spirit of my concept and story. The science component was totally missing from the film.'

Hold on. Did he just say there was supposed to be a 'science component' in a film about a creepy guy abducting a pretty girl to prevent her from marrying another man? I request him to elaborate on that point, so he is kind enough to mail me his concept note for the film which I'm reproducing word for word, without any editing and with his permission, as Appendix II (p. 226).

To my mind, the basic story outlined in the note is the same as the story of *Impatient Vivek*. I'm afraid though I don't see a 'science component' in Dr Tyagi's concept note any more than I did in the film, unless of course we are to deem every human story as an illustration of Darwin's theories on 'natural selection' and 'survival of the fittest'. Refined direction and acting plus a more mature screenplay could have made this a film worth watching, but that goes without saying, doesn't it?! C'mon doc, I mean, give the same story to two different directors, with two different screenplay writers fleshing out that story and two different sets of actors in the cast, and of course you will get two completely different films – because it's always the treatment that matters, even more than the subject. I am bursting with questions, as always. After two-and-a-half months of persistent emails, I finally manage to speak to Dr Tyagi who turns out to be an extremely pleasant person and the brother of an ex-colleague. He is most apologetic about the way he has been avoiding talking to me. When I identify myself, he says, half laughing: 'So you finally managed to get my phone number.' I reply: 'I've had it for a couple of months but I prefer not to phone someone unless they've said it's okay. I am sorry to intrude in this fashion, but I assure you, I would not have called if my deadline was not approaching.' Though he gives me his assent to print the concept note in this book, he explains that he does not wish to be interviewed on the subject because of his aversion to the film. I'm afraid I'm still not convinced about that 'science component' but...ah well, at least someone shares my anguish!

Incidentally, I've devised ways of mitigating the trauma of watching films like *Impatient Vivek.* Sometimes I've been alone in a hall and laughed out loud in the middle of an unintentionally funny flick, much to the surprise of the ushers. Yes, *that's* how hilarious a truly horrid film can be. But I've also developed a certain Bad Film Viewing Etiquette for myself:

Observation 1: If a few couples also turn up in a near-empty theatre to watch an obscure film, chances are it's not the film that's drawn them to that darkened hall. This leads to...

Rule 1: To avoid embarrassment, don't sit in the same row as any such couple. I learn this the hard way one Sunday afternoon when I plonk myself in my designated seat to watch *Hum Tum Shabana* starring Tusshar Kapoor, Minissha Lamba and Shreyas Talpade. Some seconds into munching my popcorn, it dawns on me that the love birds a few seats away stopped their passionate necking when I entered the hall. My presence has made them self-conscious and though the boy does try to light her fire a couple of times after that, I see her from the corner of my eye swatting him away. Erm...I stay awkwardly glued to my seat, afraid that I'll reveal my discomfiture and humiliate her further by changing rows...

If she's reading this now, I wonder if she'll derive any consolation from the knowledge that I too was utterly mortified!

Observation 2: The critical acclaim a lesser-known film has received is inversely proportional to the number of canoodling couples in a hall where it's being screened. Read: the more the number of positive reviews for a small film, the less the level of lust in the theatre. People rarely go for a film they're genuinely

interested in watching when their sole purpose is to make out with their partners!

Amorous couples are all in a day's work for a regular film viewer, but at a multiplex in Noida, Uttar Pradesh, one autumn afternoon, I am startled out of my wits when the woman in the row just ahead of mine begins moaning in the middle of a gloriously ghastly ghost story called *Who's There? Kaun Hai Wahan?*! I sit there diligently jotting down points for my review as I sometimes do, pretending that I haven't noticed the dozen or so couples in the hall, not one of them looking at the screen. But this particular twosome is clearly in violation of some section of the Indian Penal Code, I bet! When her groans get loud enough for others in the hall to hear, an usher comes over and chides them. Ahem…order restored – he in his seat, she in hers. Off the boy goes to do god-knows-what, then returns – coffee tray in hand – to pleasure her again in ways that no beverage can! How is a conscientious journalist to concentrate?! The usher – God bless his soul – is back, ticks them off, and hovers about in that aisle for the rest of the film, keeping an eye on them. Peace at last!

Well, my year was filled with fellas like Dr Vivek Sudershan PhD, classics like *Who's There? Kaun Hai Wahan?* and *Tension Doooor*, which leads me to…

Rule 2: When in a near-deserted movie hall, wear blinkers.

3

'An Actor Arises [sic] from Africa'

I've spent 12 months in search of this man. And after 18 years of being a journalist, I have now discovered that pinning down Amitabh Bachchan or Aamir Khan is not as tough as trying to locate the Vipinnos of the film industry.

The Vipinno bug bites me one chilly winter evening as I sit alone in a hall in Noida's Spice multiplex and hear an awkward actor wail these words out to his leading lady: 'I love you Anna!' I'm not sure whether to laugh, barf or cry at the sound of my own name emerging from this peculiar gentleman's mouth. It's the last show of the day, and if my mother knew I had foolishly risked my safety to keep my New Year resolution intact, watching a film this late at night at a theatre so far from home, I'd be in serious trouble with her! I'll think about that tomorrow, I tell myself in Scarlett O'Hara style. But first I must endure this travesty of a film.

Tum Hi To Ho is so ridiculous that I laugh out loud repeatedly, drawing curious glances from a group of ushers whose cheeky chatter about the film keeps me doubly entertained. Vipinno stars as Rajiv, a man who loses his sanity when he loses his girlfriend Anna in an accident. Sensitivity is an alien concept to this film in which a doctor calls his patient '*paagal*' (mad). In a dramatic scene often seen in 1970s Bollywood, Rajiv yells at a statue of God for giving him such a raw deal. But the Lord who responded so kindly to Amitabh Bachchan's generation, seems not to care about Vipinno. Maybe God was just furious at having his name dragged into this strange film!

When Rajiv bumps into a girl who looks exactly like his late lamented lover, he bumps off her husband and everyone else who stands between them. As the detective on the case, Jackie Shroff has a substantial supporting role in the film. As does the late Hindi and Punjabi film and TV actor Vivek Shauq, best known to us as comedian Jaspal Bhatti's regular associate in the *Ulta Pulta* and *Flop Show* television series. *Tum Hi To Ho* makes *Impatient Vivek* look classy! And Vipinno makes Vivek Sudershan seem worthy of a National Award! The only film I've seen worse than this is *Tension Doooor* of which we must speak at leisure.

Tum Hi To Ho is such an unbelievably tacky production, that in one scene I can see the ripples on a back-cloth depicting mountains in front of which the hero performs a uniquely laughable, utterly priceless song-and-dance routine. If Hrithik Roshan and Prabhu Deva are adjectives for great dancing, Vipinno is their antonym. The standee outside the hall and the film's trailer grandly announce: 'For the first time on the Indian screen, an actor arises [sic] from Africa.' That seals the deal for me – I know I will not rest till I've tracked down this man who has arisen (sic) from another continent to a-land in Bollywood!

A smattering of media reports tell me that Vipinno is a businessman from a family of Gujarati origin based in the south-east African coastal nation of Mozambique. His is the sort of film that is made on the sidelines of the industry, where top-grade PR agencies don't venture, so locating him is an arduous process. But Contact X leads me to Y who points me in the direction of Z who nudges me towards A who suggests I speak to B who gives me the number of C who finds Vipinno's telephone number in his office. I finally track him down in Zurich where he speaks to me between meetings. It turns out his full name is Vipinno Chandulal. He confirms that he is a second-generation Gujarati living in Mozambique, and vaguely says he is 'involved in several businesses including the beverage industry' but declines my request for a few basic details. His office too avoids giving me a backgrounder on his business interests, while informing me that he is the CEO of the Adil Group in Maputo, Mozambique. The 42-year-old Bollywood aspirant adds: 'I've been watching Bollywood films since my childhood and it's been a childhood dream to become an actor. I've been going to Mumbai every year on work for 5-7 years. On each trip I would set aside 2-3 days just to build contacts in the film industry. Finally, I met the director of *Tum Hi To Ho* (*THTH*) through someone.'

While hunting down Vipinno, I end up speaking to several members of Team *THTH* and discover that many of them have been associated with far more respectable and even high-profile projects in the past. They talk rather frankly about this questionable product which bears their name. The most disarming of them all perhaps is the film's story and screenplay writer Rajan Agarwal who believes that this film could have been better if it had been in better hands. Isn't he worried that associating with such a project could affect his CV? 'Nothing of the sort, Ma'am,' he replies with absolute equanimity. 'Many small actors work on big and small films. People only recognise you for your hits. If you hadn't asked me specifically about *Tum Hi To Ho*, I would have simply told you about my association with Anees Bazmee's *Ready* (2011, starring Salman Khan), *Thank You* (2011, with Akshay Kumar and Sonam Kapoor) and *No Problem* (2010, starring Sanjay Dutt, Anil Kapoor and Sushmita Sen). I would certainly not have mentioned *Tum Hi To Ho* up front.'

Although everyone linked with *THTH* who I speak to confirms that Vipinno produced the film to launch himself in Bollywood, the man himself flatly denies this. I draw my own conclusions from the fact that he claims not to know anyone from A.M.A Entertainment – the production house named in the credits of *THTH* – and is unable to 'find' the director's number for me. But the laughter inside me gradually dies down as he speaks, and I feel a twinge of sadness for this man who so genuinely believes that he has a shot at an acting career in Bollywood. 'I already have a flat in Mumbai,' he says most solemnly. 'Nowadays with flights, distances are very short, so it's easy to move around anyway. If the career goes well, I'm ready to spend most of my time in Mumbai if necessary.'

Being delusional seems like a common trait in this netherworld of inferior films. To be fair, *A Strange Love Story* is head and shoulders, lashes and eyebrows above *Tum Hi To Ho*, but the film's hero seems as out of touch with reality as Vipinno. Eddie Seth (real name: Shahram Bhagat) tells me he is the son of Suresh Bhagat who produced Salman Khan's debut film *Biwi Ho To Aisi* in 1988. The family moved to Canada for a decade in the 1990s, apparently to give the children a better education.

'We decided to kinda like go and study abroad,' says Eddie. 'So then I did my high school down there but I didn't like it too much, I didn't want to do college and I didn't know what to do. So then my dad was like, do you want to become an actor? So I was like, okay, let me try it. So then I came down here (in 2001) and started doing stuff.'

The 'stuff' includes doing the rounds of production companies where he says he got no attention since he didn't use his father's name to get appointments. I have a rollicking time talking to this young actor because like...he's like...you know kinda...like...how do I like put it?

'So my dad was like, you should mention my name you would get like, you would get some work or they would be nicer to you and everything like that,' recalls 28-year-old Eddie. 'But I was like no, because I didn't want to do something like that. For me I don't like that? I don't like the whole fact that everybody is a star kid here and no outsiders get a chance because I think outsiders can be much better actors and everything too? No, and I think it's kinda unfair because many of these star kids, their movies don't do well but they just keep getting movies you know and people who are really good, things are so difficult for them.

They have to do small roles and then maybe they'd get a chance if someone was nice enough you know. Even filmmakers that you think would, even they go for somebody who's maybe a politician's son or you know. Like it's weird.'

In 2011, Eddie made an appearance of a few seconds in *Pappu Can't Dance Saala* (starring Vinay Pathak and Neha Dhupia) which he insists on calling his 'first film'. Okay. His first full-fledged role was in *A Strange Love Story*.

Whatever be my reservations about the film, I have to agree with his take on incestuous, insular Bollywood that so rarely accepts a hero who is not from a film family. Since I've already seen *A Strange Love Story*, however, all I can do is stifle a giggle when I hear Eddie talk about talented people who don't get opportunities because of lack of connections. You see, he informs me in the same breath that *A Strange Love Story* was produced by his dad and co-directed by his brother.

The film has slick production values but it's weighed down by a truly strange script, a listless pace and its hero's listless screen presence. That said, no effort has been spared to give Eddie a solid platform in *A Strange Love Story*. Our boy plays 'world-famous photographer Kabeer' (description courtesy the film's website) who takes Jia (Riya Sen) to a lonely dargah one night where a ghost falls in love with her. My general knowledge improves greatly from the experience of watching *A Strange Love Story*. I discover, for instance, that the world is divided into humans, animals and 'another species' – ghosts – as explained rather matter-of-factly by a character in the film. Equally matter-of-fact is Jia's excuse for smoking joints when a friend berates her for the habit: 'If your mother died and your father hooked up with a girl your age, what would you do?' What indeed? With no experience whatsoever in these matters, I suppose I must accept that such a situation would drive any girl to drugs!

The spook who falls for Jia takes human form to woo her. This Jinn-nath (apparently that's the correct terminology) befriends the couple. At one point in the film, Kabeer casually tells a policeman that the fellow is not who they thought he is, 'He's a Jinn-nath.' Oh, that explains it all, the policeman replies just as casually, as though this is the sort of everyday conversation Indian policemen have.

A Strange Love Story adheres to the Indian secular ideal of '*Hindu Muslim Sikh Isai, hum sab hai bhai bhai*' (Hindus, Muslims, Sikhs and Christians are brothers)...except that they forgot to have a Sikh character in the film...but never mind that, you nitpickers!!! The heroine is a Christian who believes in 'Jijjus'. The lead couple visit Hindu, Muslim and Christian holy men to bust their *bhoot*. A Muslim character plays football with ghosts. And ultimately it's a member of the minority community whose mumbo jumbo scares the spook away.

In the midst of all these delicious proceedings, Kabeer/ Eddie gets an entire song to himself, surrounded by a group of Caucasian women. The focal point is a woman swathed in yards of a shiny fabric, flailing her arms about like some silver-winged bird.

I want to be kind. I want to tell this guileless and garrulous boy that perhaps he should consider another profession. I particularly want to tell him this when he recounts how his father did not have sufficient funds, yet spent ₹4 crore on this film, and how they lost money on it. However, it's not my place as a journalist to offer advice in the middle of an interview. And I realise that it might be pointless anyway as I listen to him rage against the industry machine, the press and the world at large. Sample this:

Eddie: ...Everybody was really scared to release at the same time as *Ready* (the Salman Khan-starrer), so we just decided, like if *Ready* is the only movie coming out we might as well come out with them, we might get theatres and have a chance. About a week before the release, the theatre people and the distributors said, oh *Ready* is taking 98 per cent of theatres. So we had like two shows in Bombay, like one in Juhu and one in like Cinemax which were like half an hour apart. So it was really bad, yeah. Then they didn't put our promos on at the right time. Then the day before I went to the theatres and they hadn't even put up the film's poster outside. So I had to go in and yell at them and they were like, oh the poster hasn't reached us yet. So like in the afternoon show 10 minutes before the show they put up the poster, right yeah this movie is showing as well. So we kind of got screwed there. I mean, if I was a star kid or something then by now I would have had the offers like coming out of nowhere, you know what I mean.

Me: So there are no offers?

Eddie: No, there are no offers. And also like they haven't really bought our film for TV. We haven't sold it for TV. It hasn't been shown on TV. And you should have read the reviews *(laughs)*. Like I've saved a few of them to put them up on the wall. Just attacking me like crazy. The whole review was like, Eddie's like this, Eddie's gay, Eddie is like lanky, Eddie is like Riya Sen's makeup man. And they said in my song I look like Jeetendra. I don't see what's wrong with Jeetendra 'cos he's kind of cool and he was a big star. So I've kept that review actually. I'm gonna put it up on my wall. He looks like Jeetendra cos he's wearing all white and God knows what, they just went crazy on me. And I think if I was a star kid they wouldn't dare. They wouldn't dare. Maybe they would write a line like he might improve, he has potential or something like that. Because I didn't have any backing so they were just taking all of their anger and all of their frustrations just out on me.

Me: But when Vashu Bhagnani launched his son Jackky Bhagnani in 2009, he got extremely bad reviews. Vashu Bhagnani is a powerful producer. So I don't think what you are saying is necessarily true.

Eddie: Okay, ya I mean that's true. But I mean I don't know. But they'll be still getting movies and you know people are still like, oh ya you know he's got potential and like that just because of his money. But if he was a star kid, if Vashu Bhagnani was an actor, I don't think they'd say anything like really bad about him. The only person I know that they really said something nasty about is Shatrughan Sinha's son. But even then it was just like a few lines here and there. Like this one was just like the full review is like Eddie's this, Eddie's that, nothing about the movie. It was kinda like personal.

As his voice peters out, I can't help feeling sorry for him and slightly ashamed at the way some of my own colleagues function. Of course personal remarks can be hurtful. I don't ask which review he is specifically referring to, but let's be clear that personal attacks are unacceptable and should be completely out of bounds for critics. Assumptions about Eddie's sexual orientation have no relevance to his performance – or the lack of it – in *A Strange Love Story*. What is relevant though is that this boy is not looking inward. After all, well-intentioned, constructive criticism too can be viewed as 'personal', if you are not open to it. If Eddie believes that critics don't reject the work of powerful people's children, if he is under the impression that Vashu Bhagnani does not count as a powerful person in the Hindi film industry although his filmography includes *Coolie No. 1, Hero No. 1, Biwi No. 1* and 2011's surprise hit *F.A.L.T.U.*, if he thinks Jackky Bhagnani does not count as a star son because his father is *merely* a producer and not an actor, if he believes that criticism of his own performance stemmed only from the fact that he is 'not a star kid', well then he's in trouble.

Eddie's second film is already in the works. *Raja Ko Rani Se Pyaar Ho Gaya* is a romantic thriller that will most probably be directed by his father. Going by Eddie's own argument against an industry where so many truly talented people struggle to get a break while children of film families are repeatedly given chances…isn't this like, kinda unfair?

You may contend that this injustice is meted out by the cosmos, not by these individuals. After all, Vivek Sudershan, Vipinno and Eddie/Shahram's family have a right to do whatever they please with their own cash. True enough, but Vivek and Vipinno's furtiveness and Eddie's roundabout arguments are hard to respect.

At least Sachiin J Joshi is not pretending. This Mumbai-based industrialist did not appear to exert a single acting muscle on his face through the entire length of his debut film *Azaan* in 2011, but who knows how far doggedness can go. You must have seen the promos of *Azaan*, even if you didn't see the film. The ₹ 4 crore budget for *A Strange Love Story* feels like small change compared to the ₹ 50 crore Sachiin blew up to produce the film that launched his Bollywood acting career. And small change it may actually be for the son of JM Joshi, *gutka* baron and Chairman of the ₹ 3,000 crore JMJ Group. Sachiin himself is Vice Chairman of the group.

Did he recover the money spent on *Azaan*? The producer-actor replies calmly: 'From a film of this scale and calibre and being a debutant, what I could garner was the recognition of great cinema. That's all I've got. I've recovered a certain amount of the cost but eventually I believe I will monetise the cost in my future productions.' And yes, he was aware that he might lose money on *Azaan*. 'Of course, it was a conscious call. It was a strategic call,' he says.

So you've gathered that there's nothing wishy washy about this 28 year old who tells me his interest in acting began when he featured in a handful of documentaries by students of the Film and Television Institute of India (FTII), Pune, when he was about 6. He joined the family business after acquiring an MBA from Preston College, London. He is said to be the brain behind XXX Energy Drink, Life packaged drinking water, Mumbai's Beatle hotel, Flamingo restaurant, One fitness hub and spa and other initiatives. Along the way, to gain 'practical experience' for the acting career he was determined to have in Bollywood, he played the leading man in three Telugu films starting with *Mounamelanoyi* (2002), *Ninu Choodaka Nenundalenu* (2003) and *Orey Pandu* (2005) which I watched in part and found that he was actually better in it than he was in *Azaan*.

Sachiin makes it clear that he intends to be a life-long multi-tasker when he says: 'I'm not a full-time actor. I'm passionate about cinema and acting and the creative process. So for me my soup, bread and butter would be my business, and I treat my cinema passion as my dessert. I'll only spend let's say 60-80 days in a year on it.'

In the interests of justice I must point out that the films I've combined in this chapter are of vastly varying quality. The star ratings I gave them on my blog may help put matters in perspective for you:

- *Tum Hi To Ho* starring Vipinno: -50 (yes, *minus* 50) stars
- *Impatient Vivek* starring Vivek Sudershan: -25 stars
- *A Strange Love Story* starring Eddie Seth: ½ star out of 5
- *Azaan* starring Sachiin J Joshi: 2 stars out of 5

Azaan is the story of two little boys who end up on different sides of the law when they become victims of political violence. One grows up to be a terrorist, the other a secret agent helping governments uncover terror plots. When India becomes the target of biological warfare, Agent Azaan Khan (Sachiin) must stop it. The film's plotline seems tailor-made for XXX Energy Drink's promotional tagline: Xperience Xtreme Xcitement.

It was shot in eight countries, and in many aspects, it is world class: the cinematography, production design and stunts are absolutely top notch. What is not top notch though is its soul. Blame that partly on the script but largely on the man without whom *Azaan* would not have happened in the first place. Sad but true...Sachiin J Joshi can't act.

It matters not. He says he has got about 80-90 film offers so far. Two films in which he plays the leading man go on the floors in 2012. He is co-producing both. *I Am Charles* is loosely based on the life of Charles Sobhraj and is being directed by Soham Shah who had earlier helmed *Kaal* starring Ajay Devgn, John Abraham, Vivek Oberoi, Lara Dutta and Esha Deol, produced by Karan Johar and Shah Rukh Khan. In another film, Sachiin plays a policeman and Mallika Sherawat is 'a queen of dance bars' with a bunch of respected character artistes including Naseeruddin Shah as co-stars. This one is being directed by Ankush Bhatt who made 2011's *Bhindi Baazaar Inc* starring Prashant Narayanan who is now best known as the misogynistic, mentally unstable serial killer and rapist of *Murder* 2 (2011). Other goals on Sachiin's checklist: direction, writing, music direction and perhaps in-film product placement.

I don't know about happiness, but money sure as hell can buy a whole lot else!

4

Who Killed The Small Film?

Just as I start worrying that this book will be a crib-athon, the tide changes. The year is not only about *Tension Doooor* and Vipinno! There is good news on the horizon! Halleluiah!

The telephone rings. It's my former colleague and fellow filmaniac Ankit. 'There's a film called *Memories In March* in theatres,' he says in his usual earnest manner. 'Please please review it.' The name is familiar. It's been mentioned in the week's newspaper listings...but it's an English film from Kolkata (not a Bollywood film) and since this New Year resolution on Bollywood films is taking up all my time, I'm not sure I'll manage to watch it right away. 'No pleeease, you *have to* see it. It's beeeeeauuutiful,' Ankit persists. 'And once you see it, you *have to* review it so that people know it's out there. It's important.'

Whoa! Okay!

So I drive over to PVR at Ambience Mall-Gurgaon that evening, to watch *Memories In March*. This Deepti Naval-

Rituparno Ghosh-Raima Sen-starrer is directed by debutant Sanjoy Nag and told in English peppered with Hindi and Bengali. I go with an open mind as always. Since I haven't spotted any coverage of the film in the Delhi press, I also go with no knowledge whatsoever of the story. I'm in for a pleasant surprise.

Memories In March is about a mother who discovers that her son was gay...*after* she loses him in a car accident. Deepti Naval brings heart-stopping restraint to the role of Arati, the middle-aged woman who is torn between love for her son, pain at losing him, confusion and hurt because there was more to his life than she was aware of. It might have been convenient to label Arati a homophobe, but neither Naval's acting, nor Nag's storytelling style, nor Ghosh's fine writing insinuates any such thing. Arati is just another older person in India whose reaction to homosexuality is governed by ignorance due to lack of exposure, not lack of sensitivity.

I can see why Ankit would urge me to watch this film. He has often told me about the prejudice and discrimination he has faced, growing up as a gay person in India. *Memories In March* is an unusual story, and could have been an important talking point in the national debate about alternate sexuality and gay rights. The film was premiered at the Busan International Film Festival, South Korea, in 2010 and won the Best English Feature Film Award at the 58th National Awards in India the same year. It was also screened at MAMI (the Mumbai Academy of Moving Images festival) in Mumbai, the International Film Festival of Kerala, Mahindra Indo-American Arts Council (MIAAC) Festival in New York where it won the Best Screenplay Award,

Durban International Film Festival in South Africa, fests in Chennai, Pune, London and elsewhere.

What's the point if non-festival-going India didn't watch it though? I come away from *Memories In March*, frustrated as always by the naïveté of well-meaning producers backing small films in our country. What's the idea behind supporting a lovely film if you don't put out a word about it? The audience can't possibly buy tickets to the film if they don't know of its existence in the first place. And worse, when such films fail, Indian audiences are blamed for not being open to new ideas!

When I vent my anger on my blog, upset at the thought of a good film being wasted in this fashion, reader ChirpySree writes in: '...Maybe the producers are satisfied with the international accolades. They don't bother enough to see if we get to know about it.'

I've calmed down considerably by the time I speak to director Sanjoy Nag many months later. *Memories In March* was produced by the Kolkata-based Shree Venkatesh Films (SVF), a production, distribution and exhibition major in eastern India. Sanjoy says that since it was SVF's first English film, they too were learning the ropes as they went along. He expresses his frustrations on another front. 'You go to a multiplex manager with a film like this, and he will give you either a 10 am slot or sometime in the afternoon on a weekday,' the 44-year-old says bitterly. 'Even Indian film festivals that are supposed to promote such films are going after big names. As a first-time filmmaker I don't expect to be the opening or closing film, but at MAMI, they had only one screening of *Memories In March*, on Monday at 11.45! Who will come at that time on a weekday in Mumbai?

Whereas at Pusan, it had nine screenings through the day plus a separate press screening. The same thing happened in Durban and New York. But in India, except probably Kerala, every other festival gives you weird timings. In India we can tell people that we have 50,000 festivals, but what's the point? Are we actually serving the purpose for which we are doing the festival? That purpose being to promote good cinema.'

The increasing monopoly of multiplexes by producers with muscle is a subject we'll discuss later in this chapter. For the moment, let's talk about marketing. I'm not for a second suggesting that *Memories In March* can or should be marketed on the same scale as mega ventures like the *Don* or *Dhoom* series. I do understand that such films are made on small budgets with little cash left for marketing, even if the producer backing them is cash rich – after all, a budget is a budget is a budget. However, if you can afford to travel to Busan and an array of other festivals, you can afford to...oh, I don't know... just off the top of my head I'd say...hold a sprinkling of early previews for the Indian press and for sample audiences who are opinion shapers on Twitter, Facebook and the blogosphere? In the Internet age, that's the least you can do for your film if you are confident about its quality. Or as documentary filmmaker Gautam Chintamani writes on my blog: 'What these producers need to do is get more proactive with some innovative marketing. A film like this could have benefited a great deal by creating a buzz on social media networks. More than anything, the lack of knowledge of screenings is killing films such as these even before they get their shot. Tragic. But more than that, stupid on the part of the producers.'

Innovation, of course, is the key, when you don't have convenient hooks like Hrithik Roshan or Priyanka Chopra in your film. Innovation though would require imaginative marketing professionals who are knowledgeable about cinema, teaming up with pro-active producers who are passionate about their product. Imagination, unfortunately, is sorely missing in the marketing of most films – big and especially small – emerging from Bollywood these days. With a few exceptions, everyone sticks to the same formula sans customisation: release promos, hold press conferences, try to get your stars invited to all prominent TV interview shows (often on a zillion shows, not just the prominent ones), get your lead cast covered on the front pages of newspaper colour supplements, send them to visit high-profile TV reality/quiz shows to talk about the film, on the weekend of the release offer them to news TV studios, and hype up the opening weekend collections as much as you can, maybe even get celebratory posters printed in advance and hold a 'success party' on Saturday/Sunday for a film that was released on Friday, irrespective of your collections, simply to sustain the hype a little longer.

Nothing in this marketing package demands out-of-the-box thinking from marketers and PR agencies *if* a film stars big names. As it happens, for such films, this formula has often proved to be an effective mix. There's nothing particularly wrong with the individual elements of the strategy either, except for the dishonesty involved in the last couple of points. Sometimes though, it jars when a production house sticks to the blueprint even when it clashes with the theme of the film, as UTV did when they sent Rani Mukerji and Vidya Balan on to a frivolous show like *Bigg Boss* to promote a sensitive subject like *No One Killed Jessica* (*NOKJ*). I must admit here that I am an occasional viewer of this intrinsically voyeuristic and sensationalist reality show. Despite that, I feel uncomfortable seeing the stars of a film like *NOKJ* on that platform.

I raise the question with Siddharth Roy Kapur, CEO, UTV Motion Pictures, over coffee one evening at the ITC Maurya, New Delhi. Siddharth, affable as ever, replies: 'That's really quite subjective. If we'd taken Sabrina Lal (Jessica Lal's sister) on the show then I'd agree with you, but we were taking the two protagonists of the film and trying to get as large an audience as possible into theatres. To our mind, a frivolous reality show with massive ratings that most of our target audience watches, is a place to showcase our film within the right context. If we had gone there and communicated that *No One Killed Jessica* was a film that it was not, then I would agree with you. But our presence there actually helped communicate to the audience that this film is coming out. As marketing people you have to take every opportunity to get your film out there as long as you're not fooling people about what your film is. As long as you're being true to what your film is, I think you have to use whatever medium is available to you.'

Fair enough. Is Bollywood being sufficiently imaginative while marketing smaller films though? Kapur concedes that the industry is struggling to figure out how to publicise films that don't have straightforward concepts or heavyweight stars. Like the engaging 2011 release *Shor in the City* from Balaji Telefilms' wing Alt Entertainment, or UTV's own 2008 release *Mumbai Meri Jaan,* a film on the aftermath of the July 2006 train bombings in Mumbai, starring Soha Ali Khan, Irrfan Khan, Paresh Rawal, Kay Kay Menon and R Madhavan.

'Your question really goes to the heart of the problem that any film industry faces worldwide,' explains Kapur. 'When you've got films that cannot be compressed into one line... *The Dirty Picture* was 'the rise and fall of a matinee sex idol Silk Smitha'. *No One Killed Jessica* was 'the fight for justice of two women on two ends of the spectrum but who came together'. *Shor in the City* – what is it? Its cast is not known, and only once you have sat through that film do you understand that it's got layers, complexity and depth. But if you had to encapsulate it into a phrase or one line and tell someone what that film is, it's very difficult. It's tough to promote a film of that nature. We at UTV faced the problem with *Mumbai Meri Jaan*. It's one of the best films we've produced. But it just didn't work at the box office and that wasn't because of lack of marketing spend or lack of trying. It was much more because the more you marketed that film, the less people wanted to watch it because it was a bleak, dark film. Only once you went through the experience of watching it would you understand what it's about. Obviously we have to think deeper about finding that one high concept or one USP within each film that we are then able to communicate to the audience. With films that don't have obvious marketing pegs, it's never going to be easy.'

Memories In March is not a Bollywood film, but it suffered from the same malaise. And *Shor in the City*, despite the might of Ektaa Kapoor's Balaji backing it, was not able to crack it either.

After my tête-à-tête with UTV's Siddharth Roy Kapur, I throw myself a challenge: could I encapsulate in one line, a film that I loved that didn't make a mark at the box office? Let's begin with the précis of *Shor in the City*'s plot that I had written in my review when the film was released:

> Ever since Ram Gopal Varma broke new ground with that amazing gangster flick *Satya* in 1998 and followed that up with the equally compelling *Company*, Bollywood has been hooked on Mumbai's underbelly. *Shor in the City* visits familiar ground but does so in a delightfully unfamiliar fashion. The film tells three partially intersecting stories. Tilak, Ramesh and Mandook are friends who are up to no good. Mandook is a loose cannon without a conscience. Ramesh has a head on his shoulders in spite of his vagabond ways. And Tilak, the most reluctantly dishonest of them all, is in the pirated books business. Far removed from their murky world is Abhay, an NRI who has returned to India to run a small enterprise and comes up against a wall of corporate inefficiency, institutional corruption and underworld interference. Somewhere in between is Sawan Murthy a.k.a. Savvy, a cricketer struggling to raise money to bribe a selector, while his girlfriend is paraded before prospective grooms by her family.

The USP of the wonderfully unpretentious *Shor in the City* was the way it seamlessly and inoffensively wove wit into the bleakness of the scenario it was visiting. So let me see if I can come up with that one-sentence description... How about 'a humorous yet despairing look at the dark side of Mumbai'? That's an accurate assessment, but not enough, I suspect, to draw audiences into halls since Mumbai has been such a common theme for Hindi films for at least a couple of decades now. And the potential of that humour+pathos blend is hard to explain. It has to be 'experienced', just as Kapur says.

Okay, how about 'Sendhil Ramamurthy's Bollywood debut'? I smile to myself even as I key in that sentence because of course Ramamurthy – star of the US TV series *Heroes* – is a pleasure to behold shirtless with a white towel wrapped around his waist in *Shor in the City*. Unfortunately he is not well known enough among Bollywood buffs in India.

Then try this: 'the best ensemble cast of the year'? Nope, that's a post-release observation not a pre-release promotional peg. Pitobash who played Mandook did go on to win the 2012 Screen Award for Best Actor In A Comic Role. And if Indian awards-givers went strictly by the globally accepted norms for Best Ensemble Cast awards, then this film should have got that prize too. But you wouldn't know that till you see the film, right?

The point I'm making here is that I *do* see the challenges involved in marketing a film with an unknown or lesser-known cast, however talented they may be...but I also think that in some cases, there are obvious steps not being taken. Besides, I'm not the marketing professional in the picture here. Devising such strategies is the job of experts. I'm just a journalist who fell in love with a small, sweet film and feels sad that most of the world does not know of it.

Shor in the City's co-director Krishna DK strikes at the root of the problem when he says: 'A film like this requires time to grow. It should not be an opening weekend film. But right now the entire industry's culture is all about the opening weekend. This is a big disadvantage for smaller films without a big star cast because these are films that need to keep playing, potentially for 6-8 weeks so that positive reviews sink in and audiences talk about the film to friends, family and everyone else they know, others come in to watch it as a consequence, and that cycle continues. Eventually the film will make money. But right now every film is given just a week to do all that. That more or less ruins its chances of becoming a hit because usually people don't rush to theatres on the opening day to catch such films. They end up watching it on DVD later.'

In earlier days, theatres gave audiences time to react to positive word of mouth from fellow film-goers. Not any more. Gone is the era of silver or golden jubilee runs and of judging a film's success by its longevity in theatres. Today each film's goal is to get as many bottoms on seats as possible on the first weekend, before viewers get distracted by the next massive film, the next new gaming fad, the next new TV show or that next cricket match. So big films use their clout to get the maximum number of screens showing their films, thus reducing the screens available to smaller films. Krishna, a US-educated software engineer who now directs films with his partner Raj Nidimoru, explains further: 'I can see that 5-10 years from now, there will be a lot more theatres and multiplexes in India and less clamouring for screen space, in which case small movies can stay on longer. But right now, if you don't open big you are pulled out in the second week. So that's a big disadvantage for a smaller film which has to survive for a longer time in theatres to catch on. I'm basing my comments on what I've observed in America and how films play there. This opening weekend frenzy that's happening in the Hindi film industry right now is also happening in America for the bigger films. They are the pioneers of this make-all-your-money-on-the-opening-weekend philosophy. Ten years back, films in India were played for 100 days and then you were counting your money, not on the opening weekend. We've imported that from the US but what we lack is the number of theatres and the number of screens they have to sustain small, non-opening films. Eventually, when the number of screens increases in India, I think there will be a lot more balance.'

Guess how much catching up India has to do though! According to industry estimates, there are just 12 screens for every million people in this country. In the USA the figure is 126 screens per million people. Oh dear!

Until that problem is solved, every small film in India will struggle for space and eyeballs. Some, like *I Am*, must also combat larger perception issues and social awkwardness that can be sorted out only by a marketing genius and time.

~

Winter has given way to spring when I find myself sitting quietly in a corner of a hall in Saket where producer-director Anirban Dhar (known to everyone as Onir) is screening *I Am* for the press and select members of the public. It's one of those films where I don't want to ruin my mood with interval chit-chat. Besides, I'm just too lost in thought and a Pepsi-and-popcorn break seems unappealing. If I weren't an unapologetic feminist, if my sister-in-law weren't a Kashmiri Pandit whose family has been through personal hell, if I did not love children, if I had never read Pinki Virani's *Bitter Chocolate* on child sexual abuse in India, if I did not have gay friends, would I feel the same way about *I Am* as I do now? I can't tell. All I know is that I am transfixed and completely moved by this unassuming film.

I Am is an omnibus celluloid volume of four short stories. The first is *I Am Afia*, about a divorced woman in Kolkata, played by Nandita Das, who wants to have a child by artificial insemination. The second is *I Am Megha*, about a Kashmiri Hindu woman (Juhi Chawla) who returns to Srinagar for the first time since her family left, and her encounter there with her Muslim friend (Manisha Koirala). *I Am Abhimanyu* is about a seemingly self-obsessed filmmaker in Bengaluru (Sanjay Suri) whose callous attitude towards everyone in his life masks his struggle to cope with memories of being sexually abused as a child. And *I Am Omar* is about a gay man in Mumbai (Rahul Bose) who is afraid to come out to his family and the tragic consequences of that fear.

The film is co-produced by Onir, Sanjay Suri and Juhi Chawla, with funds crowd-sourced on the social media. *That's* how tough it was to get money for this project. These are not subjects Bollywood usually bothers with. But *I Am* was born of passion and personal commitment. Onir himself is possibly the only openly gay filmmaker in Bollywood. And Sanjay was just 19 when his father was felled by terrorist bullets in Kashmir in 1990. Making this film was a cathartic experience, he tells me: 'We left Srinagar immediately after my father was shot. It took 18 years before I could bring myself to return for the first time to that city which was once my home. It's hard for me to put these feelings into words. I think I delayed my return for quite a while because I knew it would be difficult for me to face those memories. But of course I'm glad I went back because it turned out to be cathartic. I'm not bitter any more. I'm frustrated that Kashmir is no longer the place I grew up in. I'm hopeful that things will improve, but I'm not bitter. Still, returning to Srinagar was not easy. On the one hand, it was as though nothing had changed, like I'd never left, but it hits you when a stranger asks, "Are you a tourist?"

'My mother actually returned to Kashmir in 2006, a couple of years before I did and she's visited several times since, but she's still not been to the house we used to live in because of the circumstances in which we left. I can empathise. When I went back and knocked at the door of my own home and someone else opened the door...it's tough to explain what that is like. So in a sense *I Am Megha* is my story, but it's not mine alone. It's the story of every displaced person in the world. There is no point in remaining bitter. That's what we wanted to convey through Megha, that she returned to Srinagar filled with resentment only to realise that her friend Rubina was not happy either. The situation in the state has been a loss to everyone from all communities. That's the message of this film.'

Considering the general political apathy towards Kashmiri Pandits, the potential for controversy in the film's position on Hindu-Muslim relations in J&K, and the widespread social discomfort with homosexuality, I can see why raising cash for this film was tough. There has been talk that Juhi Chawla screened *I Am* for Aamir Khan in the hope that he would agree to back it in some manner, and that Aamir did not bite the bait. Considering that UTV calls *Delhi Belly* – a film they co-produced with Aamir – a tricky marketing proposition, I can guess how challenging a mainstream Bollywood producer might consider *I Am*.

Perhaps a committed PR agency hired a year before the film's release could have devised an effective strategy for this film. Perhaps the previews that were held well in advance for members of the film industry and other opinion makers could have been supplemented by screenings – again, well in advance – for women's organisations, Kashmiri Pandit associations, child rights NGOs and gay rights groups to create some buzz around the film. Perhaps the producers could have persuaded the more politically and socially conscious of our television anchors and editors to slot at least brief Q&As with the cast on general news-and-current-affairs shows. Sanjay Suri was, in fact, a guest on an episode of leading journalist Barkha Dutt's *We The People* on NDTV for a very illuminating discussion about Kashmiri Pandits, but the show was aired almost a month after the release of *I Am*.

The film industry's usual reaction is to point fingers at the media in all such matters but how, for instance, are senior non-film journalists to know about the existence of a minimally publicised film unless a concerted effort is made to draw their attention to it? Clearly a person like Barkha is interested in cinema on serious issues, as is evident from the fact that she invited Sanjay to be on her show. Just two years earlier in 2009, she featured Saif Ali Khan and Kareena Kapoor – the lead pair of Karan Johar's production *Kurbaan* – on an episode of her daily show *The Buck Stops Here* discussing inter-community marriages in the time of terrorism. The mere presence of *Kurbaan*'s cast on such a show immediately made the point that this was a film on a crucial political issue. For a small film like *I Am* to synchronise such media coverage with its entry into theatres would require great planning. Such planning requires an efficient PR professional coming on board possibly while the film is being written. Hiring a good PR team so much in advance requires cash... And there you go, we've come full circle!

As I agonise over these concerns, I buttonhole *I Am*'s producer-director for an interview. He is the quintessential outsider in most spaces he inhabits – a Bhutanese boy whose family of Indian origin fled to India to escape persecution in the country of his birth; a Kolkatan in his student days who now lives and works in Mumbai; winner of the National Award for Best Hindi Film presented to *I Am* in 2012, yet not quite embraced by the mainstream Hindi film industry. It's as though destiny has decreed that wherever he goes, he will be an onlooker, an observer, a resident of some alternate realm. Chances are that most of you have not yet seen *I Am*. Chances are too that you know little about Onir beyond perhaps the fact that he makes no bones about his sexual orientation.

In the preceding pages I have lamented the quality of some of the worst films I've watched in the past year. To my mind though, this book is actually a celebration of the small film, emerging talent, and people who make their own rules. Like Onir.

I Am is as fiercely independent as it gets in India. Onir and Sanjay Suri took the idea to the public on the online social media after most industry majors had rejected the concept. Clearly, Onir is not the sort to give up on his dreams easily. Don't

judge him by his self-effacing demeanour or his soft, sometimes barely audible voice. He is, to borrow his words, 'a stubborn person.' Over the years I've interviewed him several times. This conversation takes place over coffee and cookies at JW Marriott Hotel Mumbai with a man invigorated by a renewed confidence that he says only a National Award can bring:

Me: Unless a Vidya Balan wins one, there is this perception that National Awards are for arty films. So how does it help an independent filmmaker like you?

Onir: A lot of people crowd-funded *I Am* and worked in it for free or next to nothing. Considering that the film didn't perform well at the box office despite good reviews, and all the awards functions mostly did not mention us, it made a big difference when suddenly at the end of the year it got the National Award, the most precious award of the country. It's a validation of the trust and confidence that all those people placed in me. It's almost like redemption. Not that anyone ever complained about their money but it just makes everyone feel that the journey was worth it. Nothing else matters. A National Award also gives a film a second life. In the last few years, National Awards have gone to *Dabangg, Hum Tum* and other mainstream films. So, far from being perceived as an arty film, the National Award increases the reach of a small-budget film like *I Am*. After the announcement, the DVD sales went up.

Such an award also gives you as a filmmaker the courage to continue walking the same path. I've not been considered someone who can't make films, yet it's been difficult. Till the Award was announced, I was wondering how I would continue making films. How do I even ask for crowd-funding? Not only have I not recovered the money, I haven't really got any awards either – except abroad but what has always been most precious to me are Indian awards and audiences. Now with a National Award, finance becomes a little easier. Even if it doesn't, I don't give a shit now. I feel so much more energetic. I know that I can.

Me: Why did all the big studios reject *I Am?*

Onir: One, because of the short story about Omar who is a gay man. The reasons are obvious. Nobody wants to fund anything which has anything to do with sexuality and gender. The child abuse story was again a no-no. Today, anything that is perceived as thought-provoking will not get you finance unless a star is attached to the project. I was told by a big studio head that the new Indian audience has come into wealth and they want to enjoy wealth, that they are in a feel-good mood, so they only want to see feel-good cinema. One studio person told me, 'We've heard that you're working on an adaptation of *Hamlet*. So does it have a happy ending?' So you know you have people like that!

Me: A big studio person asked you if your *Hamlet* has a happy ending?!

Onir: Yes, a very very big studio in Mumbai. I think what's changed a lot is that earlier, individual producers were making films – good, bad or ugly – with a certain passion for what they were doing. Now, suddenly there are people who are doing jobs. During an interview for a documentary, one of them told me, 'I never used to watch movies till I joined a certain organisation.' How will that love for cinema come if you've not grown up watching all kinds of cinema? You only want to go back home and tell your spouse or children, 'Guess what? Today I signed Hrithik and I clicked a photograph next to him.' Stars, Excel sheets and share prices are important, but why are we ashamed of telling stories that give you a window to the world? You see an entire machinery working against such films, from the Censor Board onwards. Whenever you are doing something which is thought provoking, which is actually questioning and wanting a dialogue, everyone feels threatened, no one wants to support it.

Me: You think there is a fear of controversy? I don't mean controversy that is orchestrated by production houses to get publicity, but genuine controversy that has the potential to get a film banned because of protests by a political organisation, etc.

Onir: Everyone tells me I do controversial stories but none of my films has ever created controversy. It also depends on how you do your publicity around the film – asking for controversy or you want to just get it through so that people watch it and hate it or dislike it. So I don't really buy that. Secondly, another studio head told me something that scared me. I asked him, 'Is it always about feeding the lowest common denominator?' He said, 'Just because they are illiterate does not mean they are not wise. You've got to give the masses respect and give them what they want.' My question was very simple. A huge section of our population, in the north especially, believes that having a girl child is a curse. They strongly believe that what they believe is correct. Does that mean that you start a business on that?

Today all kinds of regressive things go in the name of entertainment. Recently I was watching this so-called feel-good, keep-your-brains-at-home, fun big film, and I was thinking that I'm facing so much trouble with the Censor Board over *I Am,* yet in this film I was watching, the Board cleared a scene in which a young son is crying and the mother says: '*Maine toh beta maanga tha, beti mil gayee.*' (I asked for a son, but got a daughter instead.) In a country like India, you pass that uncensored? Cut to the next dialogue, friend explaining the art of how to get the right person in your life: '*Har ladki ek bus ki tarah hoti hai. Chadh jaao, utar jaao, chadh jaao, utar jaao. Ek toh aisa bus hai jo ghar le jaayega, usko miss mat karo.*' (Girls are like buses. Get on, get off, get on, get off. Just make sure you don't miss that one bus that gets you home.) I wanted to throw up. And this gets a U certificate? Hello! And yet my entire satellite release of *I Am* got delayed for stupid idiotic reasons. I knew they would have a problem with a male-to-male kiss, so I cut it out on my own along with the suggestion of a blow job where I've not actually shown anything. What is there in my film that should make people cringe? These are things people should be discussing with their children. But when you have people on the Censor Board who tell you the first film they ever watched was in 2008, then you want to die. These are people making decisions!

Me: A member of the Censor Board told you that the first film they ever watched was in 2008?!

Onir: Yes. So imagine decisions are being taken by these people who tell you, 'Oh my god, the look between those two men [in *I Am*] will make people uncomfortable.' I'm sorry, your job is not that. You are uncomfortable because of your homophobia.

Cinema is supposed to be a step ahead, not behind. How will the audience grow if you feed your homophobia on to your decision making? And then there are studio heads telling me, 'We want to do a film with you but you know we should not go into *that* area.' What is *that* area? They don't even want to use the word sexuality because it's a dirty word.

Me: Is it true that Juhi Chawla screened *I Am* for Aamir Khan in the hope that he would support the film?

Onir: Yes, for Aamir and Kiran like we did for everybody else hoping to get opinion makers to talk about the film. Aamir is Juhi's friend and she was showing the film to her friends. I had called Kiran Rao as I know her. I asked for a bite and she gave a video bite to support the film. I don't know if Juhi asked Aamir to do anything for the film. I certainly did not.

Me: A lot of people find the story of the gay man in your film the most hard hitting of the four short stories, but the one that shook me up the most was the story of Megha. Why is the Hindi film industry not making more films about Kashmiri Pandits?

Onir: It was an extremely difficult story for me too because I was doing a film about Kashmiri Hindus, and getting into the blame game would be so easy. I think a lot of people are scared of that. Secondly, these films also have to do with a lot of what people have experienced and people, especially in Bombay, don't understand displacement. In Delhi, people are aware. In Bombay, we live in our own world. Unfortunately we are a country which has not even crossed over within ourselves.

People don't know what is happening in Kashmir. For me, the reason I did that story is because I am in a way a refugee myself. Plus my best friend has experienced it.

Me: You mean Sanjay Suri?

Onir: Yes. When I went to Kashmir to research for another film, those houses just haunted me. They have so many untold stories. It reminded me of when I went back to Bhutan for the first time after we left. My father was the principal of a school in Bhutan. When trouble began for Indians in the country, overnight he was told that only pure Bhutanese people can hold the post. After 25 years he was told, 'You have to become an assistant teacher now.' He's the one who built that school! Second, 10 of his Nepalese students were arrested and next day all 10 were found hanging. That's when my dad resigned and we left Bhutan suddenly in 1991. I returned in 1997. Suddenly you go to your house and someone else is staying there. I love gardening but my entire flower garden was made into a vegetable garden. When I saw the house and my father's school, I was like a fool going everywhere and crying. So I can feel the pain. I'm all for human rights, you know. The kind of violation that's happening in Kashmir pisses me off. And I'm all for freedom. But not freedom which segregates people on the basis of religion, caste, sexuality and gender. There's so much silence in our country because people are afraid to talk about the hatred and the mistrust between communities.

Me: You mean mistrust not just in Kashmir but also in the rest of India?

Onir: Yes, and we need to start addressing these issues. People are keeping quiet and the hatred has grown. We're becoming an extremely intolerant, aggressive society, and we need to talk. The problem is we don't have dialogues. The Indian government has done nothing in these last 20 years. Today's youngsters in Kashmir don't even know what happened. All they know about Kashmiri Pandits is literally like that dialogue in *I Am, 'Woh log toh bhaag gaye'* (Those people ran away) because they've not grown up with any Hindu friends. We don't make sure that people from all states mix with each other. We don't have student exchange programmes and mix up as a nation. In Europe you will see student exchange programmes happening all the time.

Again, in my film, the Censor Board took out a dialogue through which I was trying to address the north-south divide in a subtle way. When a police officer is beating up Jai, he looks at his ID card and says: 'Jai Gowda? *Tu Madrasi hai?*' (Are you a Madrasi?) So Jai says: '*Nahin* Bangalore.' (No, I'm from Bangalore.) So the policeman says: 'Bangalore-Madras *sab ek hai, sab saala idli-dosa.*' (Bangalore-Madras, it's all the same thing, all bloody idli-dosa.) And I'm sorry, that's the north Indian stand! But they were too stupid to understand that these things are important to make people understand how much it hurts when you do that to someone else. Similarly there is this very important dialogue which was an archival sound I've used in the story of Megha when she walks into the ruins – in the background you hear a voice on a mike announcing, 'Bring all the Kashmiri Pandit women and not the men.' I was made to take that out.

The Kashmiri migration happened overnight because of the fear of rape and abduction of women. The world over, the instruments of rape and abduction are used during any kind of conflict. This film was trying to talk about that and the Censor Board tells me this is derogatory to women?! Hello, this is trying to do exactly the opposite!

Me: Because we've become a society in which there's so much resentment among communities, there's the possibility that Muslims might have seen the story of Megha as being anti-Muslim and Hindus could have seen it as anti-Hindu. It has that potential. Weren't you scared of that?

Onir: I'm very conscious of these things as a person. I was once at a party where friends were talking about Muslims as '*kattus*', and I said, 'I have a lot of good friends who are Muslims and I don't like it.' They laughed at me and said I was over-reacting. I said, 'Unless you stop it, I'll walk out.' They didn't stop and I walked out. After that they never did it again. So for me it is what I sincerely believe in – I'm not here trying to do a blame game or to provide answers to a problem as huge and complex as Kashmir. All I know is I don't like what is happening. It troubles me. I see a lot of people from both sides going through anguish and we need to talk about that anguish, we need to heal these wounds. I have no answers but people are getting hurt, leading lives of hurt. You have lost homes, you are still seeing these horrible refugee camps in Jammu, and for people in Kashmir it's terrible, especially for a woman. I feel that women in any conflict situation are always the hardest hit and issues that lead to such conflict are usually created by men. It's very rare that women are the moving forces behind such conflicts. So for me it was important not only to make this film but make it from the point of view of two women because most wars are raged by men.

Me: I was about to ask you because I know that Megha's story is based on Sanjay Suri's personal story... What made you decide that instead of having a man as the protagonist, you would show a woman going back to her home in Kashmir?

Onir: I was reading an article about 200 women in the northern province of Pakistan protesting against a law that you have to have sex with your husband every fourth day otherwise you can be punished. 1,000 men surrounded them and started stoning. I had tears in my eyes thinking how fortunate I am, despite being gay or whatever, to still be born a man and be here in India. And during my trip to Kashmir for my research, I realised that I bonded with the Kashmiri women much more than the men. They were much more open. I could go beyond the barriers in their homes and I was sitting in the kitchen. Somewhere they were not threatened by me. They were chatting and they are so much more intelligent and loving than the men. And I thought, I'm going to tell their story. Anyway it's an untold story but there are always many more dimensions when it's a woman – the fact that both Megha and Rubina (Megha's Muslim friend in Kashmir) are in their 40s, both unmarried. For Megha it's because of carrying that entire baggage of being a refugee, trying to fight and struggle and having to be successful, and her entire youth is gone. Rubina was probably a good student with career dreams, but everything goes because your brother is a militant, and you are just caught up in a web of things where life just passes you by. And that is happening with so many Kashmiri women.

Me: But when I saw Rubina express anger at the Army for conducting checks on their house, I too wanted to ask her the question Megha asked her: '*Kis baat se problem hai tumhe? Army tumhare saath bura salooq kar rahi hai? India tumhara haq chheen rahi hai? Ya phir koi bhoolne nahin de raha ki tumhara bhai ek* trained *mujahideen hai?*' (What is your problem? That the Army is treating you badly? That India is snatching away your rights? That no one lets you forget that your brother is a trained *mujahideen*?) Is that an unfair question?

Onir: The reason I wanted Megha to ask that question is because sometimes when we are outside, militancy is such a stereotyped thing. You know when I was shooting I used to always think, if I was a Kashmiri woman or a Kashmiri, I think I would hate the Indian Army. Whenever a Kashmiri woman passes by, the gaze that the Indian Army guys have, they literally undress them with their look. I would not feel comfortable as a woman where every 100 feet there is someone standing and looking at you like that. I have had very important Army people coming into the shoot to meet the actors and all, and then suddenly I realise that all these young Kashmiri girls are coming with them, and then I get to know someone has a brother in prison, someone has a father, and they get exploited.

Our Army has done nothing to ensure love. I'm not saying they have an easy task, 'cos if I turn the tables… I remember once during a recce, I was clicking this Army vehicle. One of the guys caught it and said, '*Kyun marvaaoge yaar? Photo mat kheecho.*' (Why get us into trouble? Don't take pictures.) When I said, 'Okay *main* delete *karta hoon*' (I'll delete them) he said, '*Thoda baith kar baat toh karo. Yahaan koi baat hi nahin karta hum logon ke saath.*' (Won't you sit and talk to me? Nobody here ever talks to us.) You realise that these people get paid twice or something to go there, they come from far away, they're staying in this place where everyone hates them, they may die any time, they are extremely lonely and the officers live really well, but the way these people live...oh my god!

Me: You mean the lower-ranked personnel?

Onir: Yes, terrible conditions! We don't take care of them. So you know there's also that side of it. But if you are a surrendered militant, the trauma is never over. There is a certain behaviour which is constantly violating your private space and saying, 'You know we have the power, I can take you any time I want and do what I like with you. As an Army guy I have the right to slap you when I want to whether you've done anything or not.' Which is the same thing, like I feel like I belong to the minority community being a gay person in India.

Recently, there was this gay party in Bombay which was attended by many people I know. The police came in and those 400 people were brought to the *thana*, made to hold their ears and kneel down at night. There were no drugs happening there or wild sex but each one was made to pay ₹1,400 without receipts, and when they asked why, they were slapped. So as a gay person I can get slapped any time by a police officer because for him I'm a criminal. Similarly in Kashmir, because of the law, because of the way the military is powered, they can misbehave with whoever they want. So for the civilian population, it's not that the Army and the police are made to serve you, to protect you. They have the power to insult and humiliate you all the time because you are a Kashmiri Muslim. Like you are gay. I feel that.

Me: For some reason people assume that you make only gay films...

Onir: I made a mistake. During *My Brother Nikhil,* we didn't speak about Nikhil being gay till the film was released, so *My Brother Nikhil bhai-behen ki kahaani hai* (is a story about a brother and sister), little bit about AIDS came out, that was it. But when I was doing *I Am,* I thought by now the audience has also changed, there is so much more of openness in society. A total miscalculation. We spoke about all the four stories in the film, but what was picked up by the media was, oh *that* story, oh the first kiss, whatever. People didn't speak about the other stories in *I Am,* so people thought it's a gay film.

Me: There is then the possibility that a Hrithik or a Shah Rukh may decide, I don't want to act in that film by Onir because there is this perception he makes only gay films.

Onir: But of my four films, two have nothing to do with sexuality. And I have met SRK for a film long ago and it was not a gay film and it did not work out because of other reasons.

Me: But what can you do about that perception problem?

Onir: The next two films I'm producing have nothing to do with sexuality. But neither am I going to shy away from it.

It's an important part of my identity which has been violated in this country. If they are shying away from me, the next thing is I have to hide my sexuality also very soon. 'Oh he's gay, so we won't work with him,' so then maybe I should start pretending to be heterosexual. I will not do that. If I want to make a film which has elements of sexuality I will talk about it. If it does not, of course I make an extra effort to make sure that people understand. But I think it has also got to do with who I am. A lot of people are okay if you don't talk about it, but oh he's an openly gay filmmaker, to work with him?! And that way actresses I find are amazing and open, actors are not.

Me: Is this also perhaps one reason why so many filmmakers are openly gay among their circle of friends but not in public? Because the audience might say, '*Gay hai yaar, uska film nahin dekhna hai*' (He's gay so let's not watch his film)? Because heroes may say, 'It will affect my macho image if I work with him'?

Onir: There are lots of powerful filmmakers about whom everyone is aware. Some of them make very beautiful mainstream films which are loved. Being gay does not take away from the fact that I can tell a love story between a man and a woman. I don't think the audience will stop going to watch a mainstream film because the director is gay. People go despite knowing people's sexuality. You don't need to go drumming but what troubles me is that the LGBT [lesbian, gay, bisexual and transgender] movement at this point needs momentum and whether you are straight or gay, you can just support it as human rights. Vikram Seth telling openly that he is bisexual makes a difference. It just says, 'Oh, he is this? And we loved him for so long', so overnight you can't start hating that person because he's gay. So it does help you know. And how can one be living this lie? When you are in a position of strength to make a difference with the kind of films you are doing? It's absolutely okay not to do films which have gay characters but at least don't do the opposite where you harm your own community.

Me: You mean, don't make films with jokes about gay people?

Onir: Ya, as long as you're making jokes where you are laughing *along*, fine, but if you're laughing *at* all the time? Not funny.

Me: Tell me a film that's laughing *at* the gay community.

Onir: (*Laughs*) I can't take names. I'm already blacklisted by too many people because I talk too much. But very often Hindi mainstream films have over the top trans-dressers as gay characters. The only representation is that, and you're always laughing *at*. At the end of the day the word that the audience goes back home with is '*Ma ka* whatever *bigad gaya*'.

Me: *Ma da laadla bigad gaya?* (This, of course, is the title of a song from producer Karan Johar's film *Dostana* which is about two US-based Indian men – played by Abhishek Bachchan and John Abraham – who pretend to be a gay couple to get a flat on rent.)

Onir: And that is the message that goes across. You know India as a society is not homophobic. You see men walking hand in hand all over the place. But now suddenly it's *'Oh dekh, Dostana ja raha hai.'* (See, there goes *Dostana.*) Sometimes it's not even a conscious effort but people need to think. It's the same thing that when a big mainstream film has the hero trying to woo the heroine, she's not listening so carry her to the police station, tie her up, get her father there, humiliate him, he commits suicide, the girl takes her suitcase and comes to the home of the hero. What does it tell? That to woo a girl you molest her, humiliate her? And this is in a country where this is happening all the time. I'm sorry, don't do this. I have nothing against mainstream entertainment, humour or romance. All I'm saying is, do not pass off your regressive ideas as entertainment because people carry those things home. Shit ya, I'll get thrown out of the industry! (*I laugh*)

Me: Okay, so I'll be honest with you. When I watched *Bas Ek Pal,* I felt this was not a space or an idiom that comes naturally to you. I remember thinking, is this Onir's effort to be what he thinks mainstream is? (*Bas Ek Pal* was Onir's second feature film, a thriller that starred Juhi, Sanjay, Urmila Matondkar and Jimmy Sheirgill.)

Onir: I'm not proud of *Bas Ek Pal* because it's not original. It came from the Spanish book which was made into *Live Flesh* by Pedro Almodovar. Initially I tried to figure out the copyright thing and then I gave myself an excuse which I also am not proud about. I said, oh for 200 years they stole so many things of ours they've still not returned, so now we should all just destroy their things and just take it. I'm not proud of what I did. I won't do it again. The other things that didn't work for *Bas Ek Pal* was that I couldn't handle some of my actors, I fucked up the entire climax royally because I couldn't handle the action sequences because you know suddenly I was not directing the shots because the action is directed by someone else and I just didn't know how to deal with it. Also I was not producing the film so things were going totally wrong by the end. But most of all, when a subject has not originated from within you... Now when I look back, I understand what was lacking was the soul because it was inspired not by what I had experienced myself, it was a borrowed experience. It's like all the remakes happening today. They are not like the original because they are borrowed experiences.

Me: A lot of mainstream filmmakers say reviews don't make a difference.

Onir: For me they make a difference.

Me: Tell me why.

Onir: Personally (*laughs*) it breaks my heart when a reviewer... I can take criticism you know. Like you are criticising me. But it made me angry when a journalist tells that you know Onir is known for pushing the envelope but there's a limit to it and don't watch *Sorry Bhai* because it's a sin to watch it. (*Sorry Bhai* was Onir's third film. It was the story of a man who falls in love with his elder brother's fiancée, played by Chitrangda Singh. Sanjay and Sharman Joshi played the two brothers. The film also starred Shabana Azmi and Boman Irani as their parents.)

Me: Sin?

Onir: Yes, s-i-n. I'm sorry, it affects my audience because a lot of people are watching his reviews on TV. I want to hit that guy. Hate my film, trash it, but don't say it's a sin to watch. You're taking a moral stand. And that same person gave 0.5 to *I Am*. I want to meet him today, I really do. Because it matters to me, because I value what people think about my film, be it reviewers or anybody who comes up on the street and shakes my hand and says wow. I get tears in my eyes 'cos I feel happy that someone has liked my work. Second, today when you are doing a small-budget film with content, without big stars, people read reviews.

Me: So reviews make a difference commercially?

Onir: Of course. Otherwise why would I put the reviews in my advertisements for the film when it comes out? All these people who tell you it does not matter, the next day you will see four stars, three stars everything which, even if it's on some vague site, they'll put it up. So everybody knows that it has a certain value. It's most precious for us because we don't have that marketing power to cheat people, to dupe people into going and watching something that they might hate.

Me: Did the National Award for *I Am* come as a surprise?

Onir: Absolutely. I was not even going to apply for it. My sound recordist forced me to apply. My cameraman put in money (*laughs*) for the application form because I was like, 'Oh god, 5000 more? I don't have.' Now of course our print is going to the archives, and I'm so proud that it will always remain a part of our history. Nothing can be more precious than that.

Me: What was the response to your National Award from the film industry?

Onir: Except for one or two people like Vishal Bhardwaj and those I've worked with in the industry, no one wished me. It was absolute silence from most of the industry. I feel a lot of people feel, where did this guy come in from suddenly, because the entire popular awards didn't even mention *I Am*, and suddenly you come and take the most coveted award of the country? I'm a nobody, I don't belong to any camp, I don't make any studio or any family richer or happier, so there are no family celebrations happening. It kind of surprised me because it's not that I don't know people, everyone knows me.

So here's the quagmire that Bollywood's independent filmmakers are stuck in – it's the best of times and the worst of times for them right now. Larger producers are keen to acquire at least a few offbeat projects to give themselves a mixed filmography that caters to every section of the audience. Yet even the big corporates haven't quite figured out how to peddle their small films. Worse, the increasing number of multiplexes across the country has led to a false sense that small films and independent films are getting more space. The truth is that as big films get bigger, they're fighting to monopolise theatres on their opening weekends and maximise initial collections. The casualty: barely-promoted small films (even those backed by big producers) which are then given limited shows at odd hours and not necessarily in the best of theatres. More's the pity if they're of good quality because positive reviews and a good audience response to such films don't take effect immediately. By the time they sink in, the film has already been thrown out by theatre owners, to be replaced by the next mega release.

Viacom 18's acquisition, the completely star-less *Pyaar ka Punchnama* (*PKP*), is a rare exception that fell through a crack in this system in 2011. The film is about three male buddies hooking up with three women who all turn out to be mean, manipulative, calculating, cold bitches without a single redeeming feature! Allow me to be upfront and tell you I think *PKP* is a Male Chauvinist Pig film! Despite my reservations about its misogynistic script and sensibilities though, I will concede that it looks slick and features strong actors. And audiences fell for it. It had come completely unheralded to theatres but survived on the strong public reaction it received and the lucky coincidence that there were no big films that had hit the jackpot in theatres for two months preceding its release, which means viewers and theatres were starved for entertaining films. The result: *Pyaar ka Punchnama* was Bollywood's sleeper hit of the year.

Director Sanjivan Lal's *Bubble Gum* was not so fortunate. This endearing film set in 1980s Jamshedpur was about a teenager coping with the double whammy of his first crush and his resentment towards his brother with special needs. I had not heard a thing about *Bubble Gum* till the press preview held the day before its release. As it happens, it came to theatres in the month that *Delhi Belly, Murder 2, Zindagi Na Milegi Dobara* and *Singham* were already blazing a trail across the all-India box-office. Goes without saying that little *Bubble Gum* got favourable reviews but unfavourable time slots at out-of-the-way theatres, and soon died a natural death.

Bubble Gum is the first Hindi feature film from Koncept Infotenment, the entertainment arm of the ₹2,000 crore Nakoda Textiles. It's clear that Koncept has their heart in the right place or they would not have begun their Bollywood journey with such an unusually themed story. So why did the production house do virtually nothing to spread the word about their film? I gather from a conversation with producer Sushma Kaul Ravi that they were confident that critics would like *Bubble Gum*. But reviews published on Friday and Saturday on the weekend of the release clearly can't be a film's *only* weapon. Besides, theatres decide their schedules much before reviews appear in the media, and to get good show timings, any film needs to create some sort of pre-release stir especially when it's landing in the midst of mega-budget ventures raking in mega bucks at the turnstiles. So the question I need to answer before I end this book is this: are big films and poor marketing killing small films in Bollywood? Can something be done to prevent their death?

5

'To Hell With Reviews'

The telephone rings. It's Producer X, one of the Mumbai industry's most prominent names. 'Hey Anna, I believe you've just watched my movie. What do you think about it?' she asks.

Err…this is always awkward. Over the years, such phone calls have lessened because those who I've interacted with in the industry have figured that I parrot a stock answer in response to these inquiries (and I'm grateful to them for respecting my mulishness). I repeat that answer today for X's benefit with what I hope is politeness and clarity. 'Hey X, don't mind, but just as a matter of principle, if I intend to review a film, then I don't discuss it with a soul until I'm through with writing my review. And when I say anyone, I mean *anyone* from the team of the film to PR agencies, colleagues at my office, friends, family, fellow critics, *anyone*. I don't mean to be a fusspot but I hope you can understand.'

She sounds surprised. 'Oh okay, I've never called you before to check, so I didn't know this. One doesn't know for sure what the exact protocol is – am I expected to call, should I not?'

There's no particular protocol engraved in stone, I explain, this is just a practice that I stubbornly adhere to myself. 'You see, I believe everyone feels very strongly about films and film stars. So the minute you tell them what you think about a particular film, they try to convert you to their point of view whether they've seen it or not. For instance, you have produced today's film and it goes without saying that it's close to your heart. If I tell you I love it, that will be fine with you but if I tell you I did not, then you will certainly try to influence my opinion. Your intentions may be honourable but you are human and you will try. I'm not saying I *will* be influenced but that I too am human, so that's a possibility. Why risk it? My review has to be my own unadulterated opinion about a film, and it should reach my readers before I share it with anyone else.'

Poor X. I hope she doesn't think I was lecturing her. I wonder too if she thinks I'm stiff-necked and self-important. Be that as it may, no principle is worth having if you don't stick to it and if I did not bend when I was the critic for a national news channel, there's no reason why I should now when I'm a humble, independent blogger writing on a platform that's not affiliated to any media house. It's not about what my bosses think or the significance of my current writings. If only one reader out there reads you regularly, that person is precious and needs to know you can be trusted.

Over the years, I've repeated these views so often to so many people, that I think I could rattle them off in my sleep.

INTERVAL

Some people have reacted with surprise, some with amusement, some with irritation, though I must say the most entertaining reaction has come from my fellow film critic Suparna Sharma. We're having a *chai*-and-chatting session after a press preview of *Tanu Weds Manu* at an airy café at DT Star Cinemas, Saket. As you would expect from any bunch of Delhi film journalists, we're chattering obsessively about films. Suparna – who has just begun hanging out with us in recent weeks – turns to me and asks, 'What did you think of the film?' Arnab pipes up before I can speak, 'Don't ask Anna. She won't tell. She does not talk about a film to anyone until she's finished writing her review.' Suparna looks at me and shakes her head in wonderment. 'But that's like holding back your pee,' she says.

No one has ever put it quite like that, but I suppose I have to agree. Refusing to discuss a film till you've written your review is very much like holding in a bladder-full of opinions. As I do with Producer X many months later, I explain to Suparna my reasoning while I worry in my head as usual that she'll think I'm a snob. No dear reader, I'm not being weird about this – you will be surprised at the number of times people have turned borderline aggressive when I've refused to divulge my views about a film I've just seen. I'm relieved when Suparna tells me she understands…but this is not the first, and it won't be the last of the many discussions we have about the ethics of film reviewing.

~

Though I won't discuss a film with anyone *before* writing my review, I've now made it a habit to pick the brains of producers, directors and actors *after* filing my review, to ask them the questions buzzing around in my head about their work. Most of them react positively and I find that I gather many insights from these conversations. A Q&A with director Rohit Shetty after *Singham*, however, turns into less of an analysis of his film and more of a seething session against film critics in India.

I realise there's a certain intellectual class that will lynch me for this admission, or what they might consider a 'confession', but I thoroughly enjoyed *Singham*. I've been quoting the honest cop Bajirao Singham's punchline to my family to explain my obsession with journalistic integrity: *'Meri zarooratein kam hai, isliye mere zameer mein dum hai.'* (I can follow the dictates of my conscience because my needs are limited.) So I'm in a chirpy mood when I settle down for this chat. When I tell Rohit that I liked his film, he sounds startled. When I throw questions at him about the issues I had with the film though, after a point he says: 'You're behaving like a teacher, you're reminding me like [sic] my class teacher.'

Now I must tell you that Rohit is one of Bollywood's eternal nice guys. It just so happens that he's also one of the guys in the industry who passionately and openly *despises* film critics. He has told me more than once in the past that 'reviews don't matter' to him but since he brings up the subject repeatedly in interviews, I suspect that in a very private corner of his mind, he feels hurt by the fact that his films tend to get poor reviews. His industry colleagues reserve their most caustic remarks about critics for off-the-record conversations but Rohit is undeterred by concerns about diplomacy although I check with him before switching on my recorder. A passing question about reviews during this interview leads to the most elaborate discussion – some might call it an argument – that I've ever had with any filmmaker on the topic.

Me: So what is your response to the reviews you have got for *Singham?*

Rohit: To hell with them.

Me: To hell with even the positive ones?

Rohit: No, it's not that. I'm not changing my statement. I was the one who told you that *Singham* is a superhit film with one-and-a-half stars. That's what we got in most of [sic] Mumbai newspapers. It doesn't affect me because most of my films have got one-and-a-half stars, so I think I'm quite proud of myself. I'm keeping up my reputations [sic] with the critics. When you're making a commercial film, you have to be prepared for this. And it doesn't matter at all. If you're making classy cinema and if you get one-and-a-half stars, then it's a problem.

(We move on to other subjects, but much later in the conversation Rohit refers once again to the star ratings his films attract.)

Me: You keep saying it doesn't matter to you. But you have also mentioned it more than once to me. So I wonder, somewhere deep down inside do you feel bad about critics not liking your films?

Rohit: No, no, no, no. I used to feel bad a long time back. Now you know who's writing it *na*. Like I don't know the guy from *** [here he names a leading Mumbai newspaper], but my PR asked him, 'Are you a journalist?' So he said, 'No, I'm a filmmaker.' He's a 23-24 year old boy who wants to become a director. Half of them are frustrated people roaming around. Some came to become an actor, some came to become a director.

Me: But I know a lot of critics and none of the critics I know in Delhi are people who wanted to be filmmakers but became critics instead. They are all journalists who grew into the job.

Rohit: I'm talking about Mumbai. How will I know what's being printed in Delhi? Because I don't read and I don't keep a track [sic].

Me: You don't read what's written about your films in newspapers outside Mumbai?

Rohit: No, never, never. I just come to know, *itna star de diya* [they have given it these many stars], ok very good. *Kaun hai yeh? Naya hai?* [Who is this? Someone new?] Then the report comes, *woh Akshay Kumar ka dost hai. Yeh kaun hai? Yeh uska woh hai.* [...he is Akshay Kumar's friend. Who is this? He is close to so and so.] Ok, ok, very good, very good.

Me: But surely you don't think that *all* the critics in Mumbai are friends of some rival star or the other and that's why they don't like your films? Surely that can't be possible?

Rohit: No, not really. But a few of them are even scared to meet me because they know that the moment I meet them, I'm going to thrash them and go to jail for a day. It doesn't matter. See, my thing is that, of late, they don't write reviews, they make fun of you. That's not right *na*? You write the direction is wrong, the cinematography is bad, the dialogues are pathetic, but you don't have the right to make fun of anyone.

Me: But if a well-informed person were to write this doesn't work for me for x, y, z reasons, can you respect that?

Rohit: Obviously yes. If Javed Akhtar tells me *ke* Rohit Shetty you've made a bad film, I will respect and I will learn from him.

Me: I'm not talking about Javed Akhtar.

Rohit: I don't believe in critics. If you can't drive a car and you're analysing a car, it makes no sense. That's why I don't believe in critics. Who are they? From where do they come? At the end of the day when they become old, what will they say to their grandchildren? *Ki beta, poori duniya kaam kar rahi thi, hum unki buraayi kar rahe thhey. Bas, aur hum ne kuchh nahin kiya.* (Kids, while the entire world was working, we were bad-mouthing them. That's all we did.)

Note to myself: I forget to point out to him that if the ability to drive a car is a sufficient qualification to become an automobile analyst, then the equivalent qualification for a film critic would be the ability to watch a film. As I read this transcript I realise he's suggesting that only people who are involved in filmmaking should analyse films. Logically transposed then, only a person who can manufacture a car should become an automobile analyst?

Me: But how can a person who has already made films and is part of your industry be fair to you because then he or she will have worked with you, will know you, will like you, will dislike you…

Rohit: No, but who else? I'm saying, why are you analysing a film? Who are you to analyse a film? And it is so sad that because all our producers and actors are not united, we are not taking action against it. Do you know any product, forget anything else, even a Colgate is launched, it is not thrashed the same day. Only the day the film is released, there are 400 vultures already sitting. And then at the end of the day, they say *arrey*, why is it only 10 films are doing so well and why are other films not doing so well? *Arrey*, you all are the ones who are shouting on top of the voice [sic] and saying that this is a trash film. There must be followers who read your reviews and watch films, and 99.9 per cent of the time you all are wrong. Let's face it.

Me: We won't agree on this because I don't think there is such a thing as a right or wrong opinion. If you feel this way, if you feel that reviews are irrelevant, why do you preview your films for the press?

Rohit: I never do. It is my producer who gets scared and does all this.

Me: So do you object when your producer screens films for the press?

Rohit: I tell them *ke Friday ko paisa deke dekhne bolo na yaar. Tum log Friday ka show dekha karo kam se kam mera ek show full toh hoyega. Mera hi samosa khayenge, mera hi cheese bread khayenge aur meri buraayi karenge.* [I tell them to let critics spend money and watch it on Friday. If you watch the Friday show, at least one screening would be housefull. They'll feed off my *samosas*, my cheese bread, and bad-mouth me.] I'm famous in Bombay for all this. That's why I get thrashed more I believe.

I leave it at that, but 15 minutes later, Rohit is back to making self-flagellating remarks about the reviews he gets. While telling me about his film *Bol Bachchan* starring Ajay Devgn and Abhishek Bachchan he remarks: 'And again, it's a super hit film with one-and-a-half stars.'

Me: If you don't look beyond your city, you will never know what others are writing. By making generalisations about all critics based entirely on reviews by Mumbai critics, you're being extremely unfair to critics while expecting fairness from them.

Rohit: No, I'm saying *ke* why are you all writing? What happiness do you get by trashing somebody's work?

Me: Why do you assume everybody trashes?

Rohit: I'm not talking about my films. I'm talking in general. What is this job? What is this job profile? It is so sad! Somebody is working and you all are just writing. It is such a lazy job.

Me: Do you have similar objections to political analysts, business analysts, stock market analysts, book reviewers?

Rohit: For God's sake, every Friday you don't analyse Manmohan Singh.

Me: The man gets analysed every single day.

Rohit: Every Friday, there are 400 of them thrashing one film. Why? At least do it on Monday. Let the film survive and breathe for three days. You say *ke* it's a pathetic film, but do it on Monday *na*?

Me: So why does your industry woo certain critics? And all of you want them to give you good reviews so you have solo previews for a couple of them.

Rohit: There are ass-licking stars who will call up a critic and ask, 'Why did you say my performance is bad?' And then they [the critics] get a high *ke* ok this guy has called me, and then they become gods. Why do we give so much importance to them?

Me: Then you must ask within your own group, why was *Singham* previewed for a certain critic several days before the film's release so that he could write a review in advance with those four-and-a-half stars?

Rohit: He saw *Singham* three days before the release, okay? He also saw *Golmaal Returns* three days before the release and you can go back and check, he gave it one-and-a-half stars. Now what do you want to say?

Me: If critics are irrelevant, why preview it for him so much in advance?

Rohit: Anna, the day I produce the film, you'll come to know *ke* I won't keep a preview. Then you can catch hold of me. I'm saying my issue is, why don't you write it on a Monday? At least let the film breathe for three days.

Me: But once the film is released, anybody has the freedom to write anything. If you don't preview the film, a journalist has the absolute freedom to go and see it on a Friday morning and write about it. Even if critics don't, the audience does anyway on Twitter and Facebook.

Rohit: The social media is a different thing. A critic becomes a responsible person when he says something about the film in the news. Nobody from the audience will come out like

*** [here he names a prominent Mumbai-based film critic] and throw a *tamatar* on the camera. We respect that camera, we touch the feet of the camera before we start a shoot. If somebody does that for my film, I promise you I will thrash that person. I'm very straight about it. He's thrown a *tamatar* on the camera for many a film. There was a film called *Haal-e-dil* which is not my film, where *** [he names a former critic based in Mumbai] wrote in the review that one day one girl got up from her bedroom, came to the hall, asked her Papa that I want to become a heroine, so Papa went to Coffee Day and picked up two boys for his daughter and made a film. Is this right? Is this the way a review should be written?

Me: If the industry feels that critics are irrelevant, why don't they stop wooing certain critics?

Rohit: I started this conversation by saying that the industry is not united, that's why 400 people come like devils every Friday and everyone is scared of them.

Note to myself: It's past midnight, and I'm tired. I also want to finish this interview without getting into an undignified fight with my interviewee. He knows that I've been a critic myself, but I'm not sure that last remark was intentionally rude or just uttered in the heat of the moment. Anyway, I try my best to lighten the mood while refusing to relent.

Me: *Hey Ram, aapne* 'devil' *keh diya!* (Good Lord, you actually said 'devil'!) I've been a critic myself for a TV channel, and I'm not a devil. And you might say that critics are irrelevant but your industry does not think so and the audience does not think so.

Even now, when I'm not reviewing for any media organisation but only writing reviews on my personal blog, from Wednesday onwards I start getting tweets from people asking if I've seen the film and what I think about it. It's just analysis. Whether you agree or disagree is a different matter, but the analysis is the whole point of films. That's the whole fun of a film.

Rohit: My thing is Anna, today films are made on ₹ 50-60 crore unlike earlier when they were made for ₹ 6-7 crore. Earlier we had one asshole called *** [here he names a veteran Mumbai critic] writing for a newspaper *jo koi padhta nahin tha* [that no one read]. Today every paper, every channel, every website has a critic. I'm saying *ki* if the film is bad, say it on Monday morning. Because there must be people who must be following you, and maybe what you're saying is not right, maybe he opens his computer or opens the newspaper or switches on TV and he says *ki achchha,* I follow him and he's saying that the film is not worth watching, then let's not go for the film. But maybe if he would've gone for the film, he would have liked the film and we would have recovered our money.

Me: But your film is as much news as anything else. Would you ever say that though the elections happened on Friday, let the election panel discussions on TV channels happen on Monday?

Rohit: Elections are something else. I'm asking, which product is launched and the same day it's being thrashed?

Me: You asked me, is Manmohan Singh analysed and reviewed every Friday? I'm saying, he is analysed and reviewed every single day.

Rohit: See Manmohan Singh…

Me: Through all my years as a journalist, my biggest battle has been convincing my bosses that cinema is important and serious news just like anything else. To me a film release is news. And it goes against the grain of news gathering and news reporting that you say we should report about it three days later. Besides, if you feel there is a disconnect between what critics say and what the audiences like, *phir toh koi farak nahin padna chahiye*! (Then it should not make a difference.)

Rohit: I'm saying, *ho sakta hai ek crore ka business aap log kha jaate ho. Ho sakta hai na?* [It's possible that you jeopardise a crore worth of business. Isn't it possible?] And I'm saying in which country and which industry does it happen that the product is launched at 12 o'clock on a Friday and at the same time it's been thrashed.

Me: But it happens like this in every country in the world, Rohit.

Rohit: No.

Me: But in every country in the world, reviews come out on the day or the weekend the film is releasing.

The public position that Rohit takes on critics is the reason why I was highly amused when – during my research for this book – I chanced upon an old promotional trailer of *Golmaal 3* which I had long forgotten. It was filled with positive quotes strategically extracted from the reviews he had received in the press for his previous film *All The Best*. If you are in a mood for some fun, do locate that promo on the Net. At one point the words 'a great Diwali treat' have been cited from a particular

TV channel's review of *All The Best*. If you visit that channel's website though, you will find that the complete sentence in the original text actually reads: 'Shorter in length – its songs sacrificed, its action scenes trimmed – *All The Best* might have been a great Diwali treat.' Hmmm...while still on the subject of 'devils', Shakespeare did say in another context, 'The devil can cite Scripture for his purpose.' Now what was that again, Rohit? 'To hell with reviews', huh? Ya right!

This conversation was not as antagonistic as it sounds in print, so no doubt we will have other interviews in the future and I will ask Rohit about *All The Best*'s trailer some day when I get the time and the opportunity. Just for the record, the world is free to read or not read a critic's reviews. On public platforms, most members of the Hindi film industry prefer to dismiss the relevance of reviews, but in their calmer moments, they concede that reviews do contribute to the buzz surrounding a film. Some members of the public decide whether to watch a film, based on either the review of one particular critic they respect or the general trend among reviews for that film. Most people I know are like me though – they read reviews because they appreciate literature on cinema, either feeling reassured when a critic they respect happens to share their views about a film, or enjoying reading a differing opinion, noting details that the critic has cited that they themselves may have missed while watching the film. Most people also, of course, love picking bones with (my euphemism for 'abusing') reviews that don't match their own viewpoint.

I always find it quite odd when someone demands to know how I could have liked a film that ended up being a box-office flop or disliked a film that went on to earn big money. Answer: because my review is my personal opinion and perspective on a film. That's what a review always is. I don't make predictions about a film's box-office prospects; I tell you what I thought about the quality of a film and what position it occupies on the larger cinematic landscape. No one owes it to the world to like a film that a large mass of people enjoyed. Khushwant Singh has a right to say that Satyajit Ray's *Pather Panchali* put him off to sleep. You are free to look at the *Mona Lisa* and wonder at the place in history Leonardo da Vinci has earned for this ordinary, plain-looking woman who does nothing but stare into space; or you could be stunned into submission by that living, breathing creature smiling her very faint, life-like smile off that canvas. Your call.

As for those who ridicule a critic for not towing the majority line and not necessarily bowing to public opinion about a film's worth, do ask yourself: why do you not appreciate a multitude of opinions? Doesn't half the fun of the movie-going experience come from dissecting, bisecting and trisecting the film with friends afterwards? What's the point of films sans debate? When you say a critic is 'right' about a particular film, do remind yourself that what you probably mean is that her/his opinion about a film corresponds with yours.

And no, the box-office success of a film is not a factor of the film's quality alone. It is determined by numerous additional factors including the hype generated by the film's marketing, the current box-office pull of the film's stars and director, the faith the audience has in that particular production house if at all the producer's name has a place in the public mindscape, the release strategy, the timing of the release and extraneous circumstances beyond even the most powerful producer's control.

Actor Parvin Dabas learnt that from personal experience when he made his directorial debut with a charming little film called *Sahi Dhandhe Galat Bande* in 2011. The film was well received by critics but bombed at the box office owing in no small measure, Parvin believes, to the fact that on the very day of *Sahi Dhandhe*'s release, anti-corruption crusader Anna Hazare was released from New Delhi's Tihar Jail. The nation remained hooked to television news all that weekend. What chance did a small independent film stand in the face of such competition?

No producer can predict the unpredictable, but a number of them have begun to realise that timing is crucial. This is why Rohit Shetty and Ajay Devgn have consistently targeted Diwali for their film releases for a few years now; why Salman Khan now has his gaze fixed on the potential of Eid; and why Aamir Khan has made Christmas his own...because the public has the time and is in a mood to celebrate – with firecrackers, parties, movies, anything – during the festive season, and those who have received Diwali bonuses have the cash to splurge at cinema halls.

Sagar Ballary's children's film *Kaccha Limboo* will be discussed at length later in this book. By the time it was ready for release, Sagar admits that his relations with his producers – Sahara Motion Pictures – were beyond salvaging. He believes the film suffered greatly because it was released in February, which was peak exam time for its target audience. 'I begged my producers not to release it at that time but they went ahead anyway,' he laments.

And those three films I just won't stop talking about in this book – *I Am, Memories in March* and *Bubble Gum* – were victims of minimal to naught marketing. *Bubble Gum,* in addition, was poorly timed as we've already noted in the previous chapter.

So a good film review is not a prediction about a film's potential for box-office success. That is perhaps the job of an astrologer. A good review is and should only be a comment on the quality of a film. A review may guide you gently towards a small film that you may not have heard of otherwise. Reviews generate debate. Most of all, reviews are records, chronicling film history as it unfolds.

~

Okay, so that's what *I* think. But why do *you* read film reviews? I tossed some questions around on Facebook and Twitter. 'Q1: Do you read film reviews? If yes, why? As in, what purpose do reviews serve in your life? Q2: Do you read reviews to decide which films to watch? Or because you enjoy reading about films? Any other reason?' I was flooded with responses, three of which I'm reproducing below:

Geetika Sasan Bhandari on Facebook

'I mostly read reviews to get the gist of a film. I think most of us read reviews to help us decide if we want to see the film *only* when it's a film that we're dithering on. When it's a film or a cast or an actor that we want to see for sure, then we rubbish even a negative review and go see it, because our mind is already made up. So we read reviews only for the ones we're not sure about, to help nudge us in whichever direction we want to be nudged! That said, I give more weightage in my mind to the reviewers whose views usually co-relate to mine. I think we all do that.'

Ram P Singh on Twitter

'Yes, I read reviews. Duh! They help me decide if I should watch or skip. Duh again! :) For movies I have already watched, it is still fun to read reviews after the fact, to discover new interpretations. For very good, high IQ, deeply philosophical type movies, reading reviews later extends and expands the overall experience. Reviews and readers' comments also help me because I enjoy observing diverse human behaviour. I take back the two "duhs". The answers weren't obvious as I initially tried to imply.'

Aakshi Chopra on Facebook

'Yes, I do read reviews. Mostly to help me decide whether I should actually go and watch a particular film – but that is only if I completely trust the reviewer, and the review is not merely the story of the film. As a reader, one is always exposed to a lot of opinions. Some, I'm afraid, are not always unbiased. Reviews don't always mean the last word for me. I also enjoy reading them because it's interesting to dissect the film from a critical point of view. While watching a film, one may get too occupied with the story, characters etc. So reading reviews also works as a post-watching exercise that helps me go back to the film, recall specific scenes, nuances that I may have missed or had not bothered to interpret in a manner that the reviewer allows me to. Lastly, there is a whole practical purpose to reading reviews. Today, movie watching has become an expensive affair. As a working

> couple, we have only a few hours to spare. Reading reviews helps us filter crap from the real stuff. For instance, I may not have watched *Paan Singh Tomar* but for the excellent reviews the film garnered.'

As for the film industry's take on film criticism…if you are a film fan, it may be a good idea to ask producers, directors and actors why they claim that reviews don't make a difference though they also joyfully tweet links to positive reviews that come their way on Friday; and why their post-release advertisements are filled with excerpts from positive reviews if those reviews really don't matter. So far I've not got a coherent answer to that question from anyone in Bollywood. Perhaps you may have better luck.

So here's the thing… Critics and the filmmaking community will always have uneasy ties, because to acknowledge that positive reviews contribute to your happiness or your film's success is to give credence to negative reviews and admit the impact they have on your own psyche and your audience. None of this should or would bother a good film critic since that job involves only two relationships: first between the reviewer and the film, and then between the reviewer and the viewer/reader, full stop.

6

The Pimples on Your Hero's Back

Now here's where I introduce you to a new actor who could well call himself Ranbir Kapoor's guru. The name's Lakhani, Sohail Lakhani, and if you have seen him in *Bubble Gum* then you don't have to take my word for it – you know he's a talented young man. He crept up on an unsuspecting me one summer afternoon in Delhi, when the sun shone bright outside the theatre in which I discovered him shining bright on screen. Sohail has been on my mind ever since I saw him in *Bubble Gum*. I didn't know then about his Ranbir connection. He is one among the many happy surprises that this year holds for me. Each time I get weary of watching bad films because of this darned New Year resolution, along comes a film filled with children and adolescents so beautiful that I almost cry with relief! Be prepared Ranbir, Ranveer, Shahid and Imran – there's some tough competition coming your way in the coming years! And the competition goes by the names Sohail Lakhani, Taher Sutterwala, Chinmay Kambli, Delzad Sanjay Hiwale and…I hope you're taking notes, boys!

~

'Shambhu, explain pollination,' a teacher calls out. A roly-poly boy heaves himself up from his chair and replies, absolutely straight-faced: 'Miss, pollination means a nation full of pollies?' As the cheeky fellow, his entire class and their Miss all collapse in a heap of laughter, I sit there at the Films Division Auditorium where *Kaccha Limboo* is being previewed for the press and I think…uh oh, I'm in love!

Yet this film by *Bheja Fry* director Sagar Ballary does not manage to garner the attention that comes the way of Amole '*Taare Zameen Par*' Gupte's *Stanley ka Dabba* or the Salman Khan-backed *Chillar Party* in a year filled with captivating performances by children. How could it? Ballary's film is accompanied by zero publicity! Z-E-R-O! Sad, of course, because my god, those kids are killers! It's a flawed film, no doubt. What's flawless though is Ballary's handling of the dozens of children in his story about a tubby misfit in a Mumbai school.

Mainstream Bollywood directors working with adults tend to play it safe with their casting. If they don't get a big star, they try to rope in a medium star. If that does not work out either, they take a shot at getting a small star, a smaller star, a starlet, a starling, a star kid, a model, a former beauty pageant winner, a politician's child, an ex-cricketer…anyone but an unknown quantity, as far as possible! I understand the constraints with which they work. I'm not judging them. Just stating facts. If the *Harry Potter* series were to be re-made by a major production house in Bollywood, it's not outside the realm of possibility that Aamir Khan and R Madhavan or Sharman Joshi would be approached on priority to play Harry and Ron, while a debutante teenager is cast as Hermione. It's rare for big Hindi film directors to go looking for new faces that are not from film families, and when they do, those new faces they seek are usually pretty women chosen to up the glamour quotient in a film starring and focused on a major, older male star. The makers of films starring children that dot the pages of my book seem to have been far more innovative, gutsy, risk-inclined and experimental while zeroing in on their cast.

And so, Shambhu in *Kaccha Limboo* is played by an amazingly natural debutant called Taher Sutterwala. This is the story of his growing pains. The boy feels neglected by his mother (Sarika) who has married a second time and just had a baby with her new husband (Atul Kulkarni). At school he is constantly picked on by the rest of the kids. Meanwhile, he develops an unlikely friendship with a cute girl in the neighbouring school. An even more unlikely bond springs up when he runs away from home and meets the smart-talking poor kid Vitthal in a nearby locality. In the role of Vitthal is a brilliant child actor called Chinmay Kambli who is a Maharashtra State Film Award winner for the 2010 Marathi film *Jhing Chik Jhing*.

Ballary scoured Mumbai's schools to find his cast. He was determined not to seek out professional child actors for his film, but to get children who suited the roles – not just the leads, but every single child in the film. So questionnaires were sent out to schools across Mumbai. 'The questions were not the sort that required preparation or for which answers could be taken from teachers and parents,' he recalls. 'We asked silly things like "what came first, the hen or the egg?" and then went with children whose answers reflected the kind of personality we wanted them to play in the film.' What followed were auditions and workshops.

One of the actors to emerge from this laborious selection process was Armaan Malik who plays a member of the cool gang in Shambhu's school in *Kaccha Limboo*. Armaan – the good-looking now-teenaged nephew of Bollywood music director Anu Malik and son of singer-composer Daboo Malik – is himself a trained singer who has sung for 'over a 100 commercials and 20 films' (as his mother proudly tells me). He was also a finalist on Zee TV's *Sa Re Ga Ma Pa Li'l Champs* in 2006 when he was just 10. In *Kaccha Limboo,* his clear and powerful voice rings out through an alluringly child-like song that – oh how it breaks my heart to say this! – most of India has not heard because no one bothered to bring this film to the attention of the public! '*Jab yeh sitaaren, chaand se milke, karte hai mujhko ishaarein...*' Do yourself a favour. Go look for it on the Net.

The result of Team Ballary's back-breaking effort is arguably the most effortless gathering of child actors I've ever seen in a film. Unlike the precocious, chweet kids in so many Bollywood films, these children sound, talk, sing and dance like children. Considering the process Ballary went through to find them, I'm not surprised that they all perform as if they are not performing at all. It's as though they were on a reality show where someone captured the daily goings-on in their lives without telling them a camera was running. Adorable, not cutesy! That's rare!

While on the subject of *Kaccha Limboo,* there are other things you ought to know. I watched *Kaccha Limboo* on a day packed with three back-to-back press previews – that's approximately nine straight hours! By the time the third film rolled around, the hall was nearly empty. Watching films for work can be strenuous. Watching so many at one go is injurious to health, and my fellow critics were wise to leave while I laboured on, driven by my outlandish New Year resolve. I was sick by the end of the day... No no, I'm not joking or trying to take potshots at those three films I saw that day (the Priyanka Chopra-starrer *Saat Khoon Maaf, Kaccha Limboo* and *Masti Express*). I mean it quite literally – I was physically and mentally drained by the time I got home that night, weak in the stomach and suffering a migraine. Perhaps my constitution is not as strong as the rest of the world's, but clearly such obsessive film watching is not good for the body and mind. Kids, if you are reading this, don't follow mad Aunty Anna's example. Frankly, I don't see myself doing this for another year of my life!

For now though, I must persist... Another day, another film, and again my heart goes flippety flop! This time I'm watching *Stanley ka Dabba* at a preview attended by a handful of journalists in an upmarket multiplex. By the time you read this book, *Stanley*'s hero Partho Gupte will be well recognised among die-hard film buffs, and the rest of the world will know him somewhat too. His debut film was not certified a 'hit' by industry standards but producer-director Amole Gupte informs me that Fox Star Studios, which distributed the film, recovered their costs. Partho is the winner of the Screen Award for Best Child Artist 2012 and shares the National Award for Best Child Artist with the charming cast of *Chillar Party*. Amole may not have managed to make his film a box-office blockbuster, but must be commended because with the limited resources available to an independent filmmaker, he did manage to create awareness – and waves – among a certain niche crowd of offbeat film fanatics who matter in these matters! In contrast, when I tell friends and even fellow journalists about the fabulous children of the mighty Sahara Motion Pictures' *Kaccha Limboo*, all I get are blank stares, and that familiar feeling of helplessness sinks in because I know talent has lost out due to poor promotions by a producer who seems not to have cared enough.

That rant harks back to our earlier discussion about the marketing of small films which I'm afraid I will keep re-visiting. Right now though, let's direct the spotlight at Partho Gupte. Taken in as I am by this shining star and his equally superb co-stars, I'm even more taken in by the way Amole Gupte worked with them. Amole is, of course, the *Taare Zameen Par* writer who was to direct that film before Aamir Khan took over the reins. He was ultimately credited on *TZP* as 'creative director'. With *Stanley ka Dabba* – which marks his debut as a director – he ushers in a pioneering approach to filmmaking with children.

This habit of interviewing directors and actors after watching their films is proving to be a very rewarding, enjoyable and educational exercise for me as a journalist. Amole speaks

with a great sense of accomplishment – and justifiably so – about the 'humaneness' involved in the making of *Stanley ka Dabba*. There were no extended shifts for the young cast of this film, he informs me, no long work hours, no makeup on the children's faces, no artificial lights. 'When I told friends there was a possibility that the end result of the workshop could be a film, they told me I had set myself an impossible task,' he recalls. 'I mean, look at the logistics involved. But I went ahead and I can tell you that not a single one of the 500 children involved in this film skipped a single day of school to shoot.'

This revolutionary approach to filmmaking with children should be a lesson to those by-now-notorious, exploitative TV talent hunts in India that don't treat kids like kids, co-opting pushy parents into their system while the authorities look the other way. 'This is my entire goal, to ensure that a system is put in place so that children are not exploited,' Amole adds. 'This must be what Maneka Gandhi did years back, which is why a representative of the Animal Welfare Board mandatorily sits in on shoots where animals are being used. But there is no one to supervise the way children are used in films.'

As Amole continues, I discover the secret behind those utterly natural performances from the children of *Stanley*. You see, it's highly possible that at some point they had forgotten there was a camera in their midst. Amole explains that *Stanley ka Dabba* is the result of a year-and-a-half-long workshop with the children of Mumbai's Holy Family High School where he once studied and where Partho – his son who is a student elsewhere – joined in. Partho was eight when shooting started, and nine by the time it was wrapped up. Amole tells me he conducted his workshop every Saturday, in four-hour sessions in the morning with two recesses built in. When it began, he did not tell the participants he was making a film. He was not sure himself what the result would be. His brief to the boys: that camera in the classroom is simply placed there as a reminder that this is an acting workshop; now improvise. And they did. It helps that the shooting was done on a Canon EOS 7D still camera, an instrument so small compared to the large, unwieldy cameras on which feature films are conventionally shot, that it served the purpose of being unobtrusive as Amole wanted it to be. No wonder it does not feel like a film. It feels like snapshots from a real classroom. The inimitable Partho is part of our discussion. 'If we kids had known that Dad would make this into a film, we would have faked it,' he cuts in. 'We wouldn't have been natural. You know how the acting can be in films and serials, no? Like that we would have been. This way was better.' Way way better!

Not every director or actor is open to pointed questions about their film *after* its release, but most open up so splendidly that I wonder why we in the media don't do this more often and why the industry does not try to persuade us to do so either. Perhaps because in a world driven by TRPs and readership figures, it's hard to find space for intelligent reportage on cinema, and directors are not perceived as natural viewer/reader magnets; perhaps because audience members who claim in public that they want sensible film reporting don't really mean it, and in the quiet of their homes often prefer to tune in to gossip; perhaps too because film crews are keen to have their cast invited for pre-release Q&As by media outlets so that the visibility builds up a buzz around their film before it comes to theatres and translates into heftier collections; and perhaps because interviews before a film's release are less challenging for the film's team because a journalist who is yet to see your film can't ask specific questions that have the potential to be uncomfortable. It's so much easier instead to give interviews before a film's release when the media's questions tend to be generic and then complain: 'Uff, these journalists always ask the same old questions!'

I mean, it takes a person with Sanjay Suri's strength of conviction to respond with equanimity when I ask if Manisha Koirala got her Kashmiri accent wrong in *I Am*. It takes the self-assurance of a Priyanka Chopra to calmly address my concerns about the quality of her makeup in *Saat Khoon Maaf*, and also to admit that the shot of a nude back in the film's seduction scene featured a body double (PC auditioned numerous backs for that scene, to get just the right one that would suit the 50-plus woman she was supposed to be at that point in the story). And it takes the sense of humour and self-confidence of a Mohit Suri to deal with my inquiry about the pimples that were showing on Emraan Hashmi's torso during a love-making scene in *Murder 2*. Mohit bursts out laughing at the question and I have to repeat myself, at which point he replies (almost admiringly I'd like to believe): '*How* closely did you watch my film?!'

Very closely! As closely as I watched *Chillar Party* at Films Division Auditorium, a regular haunt of all the capital's film critics. *Chillar Party* is a minuscule children's film co-produced by UTV Spotboy and Salman Khan. When directors Nitesh

Tiwari and Vikas Bahl (the former UTV Spotboy COO) finished shooting it, they screened it for several friends and acquaintances in Mumbai simply to gauge the industry's response. Salman saw the film at one such screening and was so impressed that he came on board as a producer. Just having his name associated with it put the spotlight on what might otherwise have ended up being yet another widely ignored flick. When Ranbir Kapoor saw it and offered to throw his weight behind it too, the directors shot the item song 'Tai tai phiss' with him and the children to run with the end credits.

Chillar Party is the story of a bunch of friends aged 4-11 in a middle-class housing complex in Mumbai. They are the '*chillar* (small change) party' of the film's title. The gang runs a national campaign culminating in a *chaddi* (underwear) march to save their friend, the car-wash boy Phatka's dog from the machinations of an evil politician. By the time I finish watching it, I'm convinced that if a children's film gets its casting right, half the battle is won even before the cameras have rolled.

To be honest, *Chillar Party* is not my favourite children's film or children-starring film of the year gone by. I found those images of underwear-clad children being bandied about somewhat exploitative. I was disturbed by the gender imbalance in the film. I'm also bemused and confused when I hear Nitesh Tiwari's seemingly well-meaning explanation for why the lead gang was all-male (there's a girl who chips in with an idea, but she's not really part of the gang). Apparently there was to be one girl in the group but two days before shooting began, the actress in question broke her leg and had to be left out. But, 'the predominant reason why there weren't many female characters was because these kids like cricket and are outgoing, so even the girl character we planned was a little tomboyish. Once the actress hurt herself, we didn't feel like adding any more girls because we already had a *chaddi* march in the film which obviously a girl can't be a part of.'

Me: If little boys aged 4-11 can be paraded around in their briefs, why not girls of the same age group?

Nitesh: Girls at that age would not step out like that. But it's not just a question of whether little girls are more conscious than little boys. It's also that showing girls in their *chaddi*s would have evoked unnecessary reactions. You put a three-year-old girl in a bathtub in a Pears commercial and it gets banned. People take objection. How can you show a topless girl? So why take that chance?

Me: So did you exclude girls from the *chaddi* march because you were uncomfortable with showing little girls in those scenes? Or were you concerned about offending people, or about upsetting the Censor Board?

Nitesh: Even if the public and the Censors had said it's okay, we wouldn't have done it because our conscience wouldn't have allowed us to show topless girls, however small they are. For boys it is fine, not for girls. No matter how liberated we are in our country, we are still conservative in our approach. You can call me conservative but I don't care. My conscience wouldn't have allowed me to show a girl in a *chaddi*.

I'm not saying you're conservative, Nitesh. I'm saying that I felt uneasy about the visuals of those boys marching down the streets in their underwear, particularly because it was touted as the highlight of the film and those images were used in the posters to promote the film. It's like this...when your baby waddles around the house in her/his panties, you may find it cute and coo over her/him, but should you put up similar photographs on Facebook knowing that there are creepy voyeurs out there who do not necessarily look at children with the same eyes as you do? Paedophilia is not an alien term to us any more. And I'm as concerned about the exploitation of little boys as I am of little girls, so I'm worried that there is a double standard at play somewhere here. Don't get me wrong, Nitesh, I know you mean well, but I hope you can understand my concerns too.

The National Awards jury of 2011 named *Chillar Party* the Best Children's Film of the year but I'm happy to debate this issue with them. One thing is beyond debate though – the children of *Chillar Party* are remarkable!

Casting director Mukesh Chhabra, I'm told, roamed the country for over two months to locate this impeccable band of *bachchas*. He went to small towns, got out on the streets looking for kids, especially a boy who could play Phatka. After this gruelling process, the directors were handed close to 7,000 DVDs of auditions to make a shortlist!

And how did Mukesh find Irrfan Khan who plays Phatka? Now here's an interesting story: 'Irrfan lives in one of Mumbai's small shanties somewhere near Jogeshwari. His casting was pretty unusual because Mukesh found him on a road,' recalls Nitesh. 'There's a funny incident to it you know. When Mukesh went and introduced himself to Irrfan, the boy thought maybe he was a kidnapper. He didn't give him his right name. He was trying to mislead Mukesh into believing he's somebody else. When he did come to meet us at our office, he came with 5-6 friends. What appealed to us the most about him is that his voice is slightly older than his face. We were not very sure of his acting skills at the time. But that voice-and-face combination was very appealing.'

Any doubts about Irrfan's acting abilities would be laid to rest when you see *Chillar Party*. At a ceremony in May 2012, Irrfan received his National Award for Best Child Artist that he shares with Partho Gupte of *Stanley ka Dabba* and his own *Chillar* co-stars Sanath Menon, Rohan Grover, Naman Jain, Aarav Khanna, Vishesh Tiwari, Chinmai Chandranshuh, Vedant Desai, Shriya Sharma and Divij Handa.

And for that, congratulations and kudos to you Mukesh, Nitesh and Vikas!

~

The youngsters I encounter next are not as young as the *Chillar* children, but they're equally gifted. As a bonus, they're blessed with lines that don't make them sound affected the way so many Hindi film children do. I almost miss discovering them though, one frenetically crazy, preposterously busy Thursday when it turns out that I may have packed too much into my diary for a single day. It's that blasted New Year resolution again!

The newspaper listings have for seven days now been featuring a film called *Chhuttanki* starring Puneet Issar. It's an unknown film and it's unlikely to remain in theatres for another week. If I don't watch it on Thursday (today), I'll miss it because theatre schedules will change on Friday. And then what becomes of that foolhardy January resolve?!

Tiny problem: Delhi is HUGE, and *Chhuttanki* is running in just one theatre in one show about 50 km away from my house. The theatre seems not to have an online booking facility and no one picks up their phone either. Damn! But a girl's gotta do what a girl's gotta do. So I bravely wake up early. Having armed myself the previous day with directions from my ex-colleague and West Delhi dweller, Garema, I drive off at 8 am to pay my first ever visit to Movietime multiplex in Rajouri Garden.

I'm well in time. 'One ticket for *Chhuttanki,* please.' 'That film's not running here, Ma'am,' replies the boy at the ticket counter. Err…but it's in the listings. He looks helplessly around at the crowd of noisy youngsters queued up behind me and directs me to the manager's room. The gentleman in question has not yet arrived and when I say I'll wait, a representative in his office gets antsy with me. Now, I'm not the sort of journalist to throw my weight around, but as a customer who has been wronged, I do believe I have a right to expect at least a show of penitence and a pretence at an apology, if nothing else. What I don't expect is this fellow who dismissively tells me that newspaper listings are not the responsibility of individual movie halls but of the film's distributor, and that's where I should be addressing my grievances. Whaaaaaat?! So he doesn't care if a patron has been inconvenienced? 'Not my problem,' he shrugs.

Hell hath no fury like a dedicated film follower scorned by a haughty multiplex staffer. I demand to speak to his manager even as I begin giving vent to my anger on Twitter. The manager is on the phone requesting me to wait till he arrives, but since his colleague continues to be snooty, I keep tweeting my anger against #MovietimeRajouriGarden incessantly through my cellphone. The manager finally arrives, apologising profusely for his teammate's behaviour and also for the trouble caused to me. It turns out that *Chhuttanki*'s print did not arrive in Delhi the previous Friday, but by then Movietime's schedule had already been prepared. So for seven days, though this film was listed against Movietime's name in the city's newspapers, another film was running in its place. I'm furious but this is also a learning experience for me. The manager tells me that it is indeed true that distributors – not theatre owners – are the ones who send listings to newspapers.

I am in no mood to verify the information at this point, but I do wonder: Doesn't it harm the theatre's reputation if customers like me come all the way to find that the schedule printed in the papers is wrong? 'Yes it does,' he replies, 'I know for sure that you, for instance, will never want to come here again. I know too that the comments you've written on the Internet will spoil our name, but I'm helpless in this matter. How can I make it up to you, Ma'am? Please pick any other film that's running here right now and I'll offer you a free ticket as compensation for the inconvenience caused to you.'

It turns out that I've watched every single other film playing in Movietime that day...except for one. And that's the story of how I came to watch *Harry Potter aur Maut ke Tohfey* (the Hindi dubbed version of *Harry Potter and the Deathly Hallows:*

Part 2) and learnt that Professor Dumbledore's pensieve is called *smriti-paatra* (vessel of memories) in Hindi.

I'm tired already and there are three film previews to follow in the afternoon. Maybe, I think, I'll skip the first one and watch it after its release. I've never heard of *Bubble Gum*, anyway. Something makes me change my mind, and boy am I glad I did!

Bubble Gum is an uncommon Hindi film. It stars children but it seems made for adults. The teenaged hero is coping with his first crush when the film starts, but by the time the end credits roll, the lasting theme is sibling rivalry in a household where parents struggle with the needs of one child who is speech and hearing impaired while unwittingly neglecting the other. It's the sort of film designed to make grown-ups ache for the lost innocence of our younger days.

Set in 1980s Jamshedpur, *Bubble Gum* stars Delzad Sanjay Hiwale as 14-year-old Vedant who has just fallen for his neighbour Jenny (Apoorva Arora) when his brother Vidur (Sohail Lakhani) comes home from boarding school on a Holi break. I sigh a thousand sighs each time I think of those children! Director Sanjivan Lal tells me that casting director Honey Trehan spent 2-3 months to find them. 'I was very clear in my mind that I wanted fresh faces and real normal-looking children, not the chocolatey types who regularly appear in commercials,' he says. 'I went in for small-town girls and boys who retain their innocence, unlike kids in metros who are exposed to too much and are sometimes too smart and cheeky. In fact, since the film is set in a cosmopolitan town like Jamshedpur where people from all parts of the country come to work for the Tatas, and they all speak Hindi with the influence of their mother tongue, I wanted actors from all over the country. And I wanted each of them to seem real with all the right accents without sounding like caricatures. So Partho, the Bengali boy in the group, is played by Harshvardhan Poddar from Kolkata. Ratan, the Bihari boy who troubles Vedant, is played by Suraj Singh from Patna. Jenny is a Christian but I didn't want her to sound like the typical Hindi film Sandra-from-Bandra, so we chose Apoorva who Honey's assistant spotted with a theatre group in Delhi. Delzad is from Pune. And fortunately for me, we found Sohail in Bombay.

'Sohail is hearing impaired in real life too. In the past we've seen hearing actors like Shreyas Talpade, Nana Patekar and Sanjeev Kumar play hearing-impaired people in films but getting a real person playing the part was important to me because the facial expressions and body language had to be just right. I didn't want to mock him or make fun of him in any way. And luckily he was also good looking.' Sanjivan's elder brother and sister-in-law are deaf, so he drew on his own personal experiences in his interactions with Sohail. The result is there for everyone to see on screen.

But what's the point, I wonder despairingly. Sanjivan tells me the film's publicity began about a fortnight before its release. That's a terribly tiny period for a film of this sort to demarcate for its promotions. But worse, who heard the message and what exactly was it? Just outside the preview theatre is a poster of *Bubble Gum* that shows Vedant showering flower petals on a coy-looking Jenny. Vidur is nowhere in the picture. The impression created is that this is a teenaged romance. It's only once I see the film that I know better – it's really about the two brothers. Sanjivan hits the nail on the head when he says bitterly: 'Any Tom, Dick or Harry can market a film with Shah Rukh Khan. There's nothing needed to be done for such a film. But when the so-called marketing professional assigned to a small film does not understand it in the first place, then nothing can be done.'

Something good may still come of this film. Sohail Lakhani was a teenager when he shot for *Bubble Gum* in 2010. He has since trained Ranbir Kapoor for his role in *Barfi*. And he hopes to become a full-time actor himself. Interviewing him presents an interesting challenge for me since I'm based in Delhi, he's in Mumbai; I don't know sign language so being in the same city wouldn't help much either, and my effort to initiate an SMS exchange with him fails miserably. Finally producer Sushma Kaul Ravi offers to be an intermediary, so I e-mail a list of questions to her and she e-mails Sohail's responses back to me: So how did it come about that you trained Ranbir for *Barfi*? Is he a quick learner? And are you a good teacher, Sohail? 'The director of *Barfi* came to our college and my teachers represented me to him,' Sohail replies. 'Training Ranbir was a great experience for me. He is a very good learner. Am I a good teacher? I must leave Ranbir to answer that question.'

So many dreams ride on every film that gets made. Those who fail to market good films brimming with talent may not realise how many people they're letting down. When I ask Sohail about his family and his own reaction to *Bubble Gum*, he writes, 'My family is small. My father died early. My mother and sister are also deaf. They felt very proud of me and very good when they saw me in *Bubble Gum*... I myself liked the film very much. I was both overjoyed and tense while watching it. Overjoyed because it's my first film and tense because I was worried about how people would react and whether they would accept me.'

Sadly, not many people have seen *Bubble Gum*, but as one of the few who has, may I just say...you bet you've been accepted, young man!

~

I suspect I will run out of adjectives by the time I wind up this chapter. The Films Division Auditorium is unusually crowded for the preview of *I Am Kalam* because the film's producer Smile Foundation has packed it with not just journalists but also with friends and associates. If you preview an offbeat film, this is the way to do it – an entire week before the release, in the hope that the large gathering of non-journalists will circulate their views about the film through the social media and drawing-room conversations. Radio spots on *I Am Kalam* have been getting repeat play in Delhi for days now. In this piracy-ridden nation, it's not the best of ideas to release a film in theatres more than a year after it was first screened at an international film festival and then toured the world, but Smile Foundation is doing many other things right. The film, unfortunately, has been available on YouTube for a while by the time it comes to theatres, but at least Smile is being enthusiastic in its promotions for *I Am Kalam* which has already won the National Award for Best Child Artist for leading little man Harsh Mayar.

The story of a *dhaba* boy in Rajasthan with aspirations to greater things in life is marked by debutant director Nila

Madhab Panda's natural storytelling style and excellent performances by Mayar (who was 10 years old when the film was shot) and Husaan Saad who plays his friend in the film. Over the years, I've come to the conclusion that great performances are a result of great scripts and great chemistry, not between co-stars but between directors and their actors. So this time for my post-release interview, I meet Harsh with Madhab to observe their bond. The interview takes place at the director's office in Delhi's congested Shahpurjat area. It's been a few months since I exchanged a couple of words with Harsh at that preview theatre in July and I can see that he's already grown taller in this short period. That's what 14-year-olds do!

He's a feisty fellow, this son of a tentwallah who lives in a resettlement colony in Delhi. His mother sits in the room outside while he chats with me in the company of his director, about *I Am Kalam*, his second film *Jal Bin Jalpari* and his future plans. So did he and Husaan get along well? 'Yes, Husaan is a good friend...,' Harsh starts off, but Madhab cuts in with a laugh. 'Tell the truth!' he says before turning to me: 'Actually they can't tolerate each other.' I can't help a chuckle myself. 'Did the PR agency tell you to tell journalists that Husaan is your friend?' I ask Harsh who is now looking sheepish. '*Nahin, achcha dost toh shuru se hi tha, par thodi si nok-jhok hoti thi...*' (No, he was a good friend from the start, but we had minor differences...) But but but...I smile at this auspicious start to our interview.

As we chat over tea for a couple of hours, I discover that Harsh had earlier been shortlisted to play Phatka in *Chillar Party*. He's been acting in Hindi plays in Delhi since the age of five and has auditioned for numerous TV shows, ads and films. 'I had been for about 150 auditions before I was approached for *I Am Kalam*. By then I was very disheartened,' he says. 'I used to listen to sad music all the time...that was my state of mind.'

Madhab: The day he came for an audition here, I was passing by and I remember hearing him ask one of my assistants: '*Sach mein koi film ho raha hai ki aise hi kar rahey hai? Bewakoof banaane ke liye bulaaya hai kya?*' [Are you actually making a film or have you called me here to make a fool of me?] Imagine what that made me feel. Here I am, a director making my first feature film, and a kid is throwing tantrums in my office! So I told my assistant, *Bhagao isey* [get him out of here], but the next day I said, *Bachcha itna bada sawaal kar sakta hai to bulaao usey* [If he can dare to ask such a question, then call him back] because I realised he must be special.

Harsh: *Bas main bahut* frustrate *ho chuka tha Chillar Party ki* audition *ki wajah se.* [I was terribly frustrated because of *Chillar Party*'s audition.] When I met Sir and he told me he's making a film set in Rajasthan, I thought it must be some small film.

Madhab: *Uska mann nahin kar raha tha yeh film karne ke liye kyunki usko laga, hoga koi Doordarshan-type ki film, chhota mota. Uska* major *sawaal tha: 'Kabhi* release *hogi yeh film?*' (He wasn't very keen to do this film because he thought it's a small film that would be shown only on Doordarshan. His big question was: 'Will this film ever get released?')

Harsh: That's because it was already two years since we'd finished shooting for it.

Madhab: No no, he was asking even during the shooting, will this film ever get completed, will it be released?

I sip my tea and quietly listen to the banter between the two, occasionally tossing in a question. Working with children is clearly a challenge in any situation. But Madhab had his work cut out when he selected the full-blooded Mr Harsh Mayar for his film. 'One of my assistants warned me on the first day of the shoot that I was making a mistake by casting him,' the director recalls, much to Harsh's amusement. Those who have seen *I Am Kalam* will remember the scene in which a very distraught Chhotu gives vent to his pent-up emotions by maniacally playing the *khartal* (a traditional percussion instrument) alone in the desert in the middle of the night. It's a hard-hitting scene and a good example of an actor's versatility being showcased within one film. Through the rest of *I Am Kalam,* you may wonder if Harsh is merely being his spirited self in front of the camera but in that one night-time scene, you see his ability to be someone else too.

Extracting that performance from the child was not easy. Harsh recalls: 'Sir told me I would have to cry in the scene, so I said, Sir, how will I cry unless you shout at me?' I'm uncertain of the political correctness of Madhab's description of that evening, so hear it in his own words. 'It was a magic hour shoot,' the director points out. 'In the evening you get only half an hour's light in which we absolutely had to shoot otherwise I would have had to set up 10-20 lights. Besides, we were shooting in an army cantonment area without permission and if we had stayed half an hour longer, we would have all been in jail, and that too with a foreigner in our cast who didn't have a working visa. *Ek thhoda sa* hero *hai hamara* Harsh. [Our Harsh is a bit of a hero.] He was wasting time doing hero-*giri* with the village children and I knew I would have to do something drastic to get the work done. So I ran up to him in a rage and shouted so loudly with my hand raised as if I were about to hit him, and I yelled so seriously that I lost my voice. Everyone on the set fell silent and Harsh started crying. He gave a great shot right after that, and later when I apologised to him, he said: "*Aap kya mere ko bewakoof samajhte ho? Mere ko pehle se pata tha aap jaanboojhke yeh kar rahey ho taaki main roney lagoo!*" [Do you think I am such a fool that I didn't realise you yelled deliberately to make me cry for the shot?] So he's far smarter than any of us.'

I bring up the subject of humaneness that Amole Gupte had discussed in the context of *Stanley ka Dabba*. Would Madhab consider the long-drawn-out process adopted by Amole to make his film? 'No,' comes the reply, 'I would not have the funds and the time to work in a similar fashion.' All the same, Madhab assures me that he's tried his best to ensure that the children of *I Am Kalam* and his second feature film *Jal Bin Jalpari* (starring Harsh in a negative role) barely missed any schooldays.

For his part, Harsh is determined to become a professional actor when he grows up. If enough films come his way, he would love to move to Mumbai right away and work while attending school and college there. His parents are apparently willing to shift for the sake of his career, but leaving school or skipping college are out of the question says the clear-headed teenager. 'Why would I quit studies for films?' he asks incredulously. '*Film apni jagah hai, padhaai apni jagah hai.* Life *mein padhaai bahut zaroori hai.* [Films and education have their own place. Education is very important.] The other day I saw on the Filmfare Awards that Aruna Irani was saying, "*Main anpadh hoon.*" [I'm illiterate.] If you're not educated, people may not say anything to your face, but they will mock you behind your back, they'll say *anpadh hai, ban toh gaya star lekin utthne baitthne ki tameez nahin hai.* [He's illiterate. He may have become a star but he lacks culture.] That's why I want to study.'

I nod in agreement at the wisdom of his words... but I suppress a smile when, just as we're concluding our conversation, he refers to himself in the third person in true starry fashion. 'If I become a big star, I want to do big films,' he says. 'I will do small films only with Sir, not with anyone else. I will of course work with Sir because *unhone itna sahara diya, nahin toh Harsh abhi bhi galiyon mein rehta, aisa kuch.* [If Sir hadn't given me a break, I would have been a nobody.] With Sir, I'll be willing to work for free if I have to.'

So what was that I was saying at the start of this chapter? Oh yes...Ranbir, Ranveer, Shahid and Imran...don't say I didn't warn you!

Postscript: By now I've arrived at a checklist of reassurances that perhaps all of us should insist on in discussions about films starring children:

1. Have the children missed school for this shoot?
2. Did they work longer than 2-4 hours a day?

3. Were they treated with kindness?
4. Have they been shot tastefully?
5. Has the child's body been exploited in any way?
6. Is the film child-like or childish?
7. Did the director look for known faces that could put the spotlight on the film or for children who were right for the roles?
8. Are the children acting because they want to or are they being forced to?

And most of all

9. Did the children have fun?

7

Who's That Girl Who's Not On Your Poster?

You know the Khans, Vidya Balan, Katrina Kaif, Kareena Kapoor and Priyanka Chopra. Even if you don't remember their names, I suspect if I showed you photographs, you'd recognise Poorna Jagannathan who played Imran Khan's new girlfriend in *Delhi Belly*, Swara Bhaskar who was Kangna Ranaut's best buddy in *Tanu Weds Manu* and Chandan Roy Sanyal who was *Kaminey*'s Mikhail and Jackky Bhagnani's eccentric pal in *F.A.L.T.U.*

But I ask you this, all you regular Hindi film viewers: do you know Maddalsa Sharma?

There is something to be said for my insane determination not to skip a single Hindi film released in an entire year. More than anything else, this resolve drives home to me the point that in every bad film I watch, there is the possibility of spotting an actor who deserves better; that every film industry has its share of films in which supporting performers have stolen the show from the lead players, and Bollywood is no different; but that star-struck Bollywood in particular is filled with supporting actors who are not considered marquee names or given sufficient opportunities to play the hero or heroine although they have consistently delivered performances that make a lasting impression even in the smallest roles; and – on a more positive note – that today's Bollywood is perhaps a better place to be in than the past many decades have been for such actors.

Now allow me to take you back to the early days of the (mis)adventure that inspired this book... The guy at the counter at PVR-Ambience Mall, Gurgaon, looks most apologetic as he explains why he can't run the scheduled show of *Aashiqui.in*: 'Ma'am you are the only person who has come to watch it, and the theatre spends more money than it earns from running a show when just one ticket has been sold.' It's still early days for me with this New Year resolution, so I am neither aware of my rights nor practised enough to get assertive. Besides, the manager on duty is a friendly fellow who has been helpful in the past, so I offer to buy two tickets to the film. As it turns out, *Aashiqui.in* is not worth the price of even one!

Aaargh! So here I am seated alone in the hall watching a dull, very literal modern-day take on the old Cinderella story. The costumes, makeup and most of the cast are below the standard of many high-school plays that I've seen. On second thoughts, the price of two tickets is nothing compared to the value of these priceless lyrics in a song that runs with the end credits, that could give primary-school kids a run for their money:

Black Cinderella, *chura le mera dil* /
Black Cinderella, *kahin na kahin mil* /
Black Cinderella, *tu hai sabse rangeen* /
Black Cinderella, just come and be my queen.

Roughly translated, that's 'Black Cinderella, come steal my heart / Black Cinderella, meet me somewhere / Black Cinderella, you are the most colourful one of all...' Hmm, come to think of it, I'd have paid for a third ticket just for a chance to read the tagline on the poster outside: '*Aashiqui.in* – Love Makes Time Pass... Time Makes Love Pass.' The film is not a story of unrequited love but some day I'll figure out what those profound words were alluding to!

All is not lost though. Heroine Ankita Srivastava plays the 'Black Cinderella' of the film. Read: hers is a Cinderella story with the added twist that since she's ordinary looking, she is not considered beautiful by her Prince. 'Ordinary looking' by this film's definition seems to mean dark skinned since I see nothing 'ordinary' about Ankita, attractive and self-assured as she is, and far far more impactful than the white-skinned (hence 'good looking' by this film's standards I guess) actress playing the ex-girlfriend of Cinderella's Prince.

Despite the inaneness and the wannabe-wisdom of the goings-on around her, Ankita seems like she ought to be in a better place. So I google her and discover her name on the cast list of Zee TV's *Do Saheliyaan: Kismat ki Kathputaliyaan* (now off air) and a couple of other serials. I'm not much of a follower of Hindi fiction programmes but Varnika, my reference guide on all matters related to Hindi shows, tells me that Ankita is yet to establish herself as a TV star though she would perhaps be a recognisable face – not a recognisable name – to regular viewers of TV soaps. The road to Bollywood is populated with TV actors big and small, struggling to make it in films. And it must be for the likes of Ankita in *Aashiqui.in* that Bob Dylan sang: 'But what's a sweetheart like you doin' in a dump like this?'

If you're a film critic, you're probably used to hearing people say you have a 'fun' and 'easy' job. Ya sure! Try being a reviewer held to account for every single word you write about a film and vilely abused by fans of some stars if you are even remotely critical of her/his work. Try being a conscientious critic who is so particular about not missing a single second of a film you have to review, that SMSing and visiting the washroom during the show are a complete no-no. And the next time someone tells you that film reviewing is a lark, please show them this chapter in my book. Try being me, subjecting myself to both *Aashiqui.in* and *Angel* on the very same day! I thank my stars that in the afternoon I attended the press preview of the mellow Nicole Kidman-Aaron Eckhart-starrer *Rabbit Hole*, giving my senses a break from the morning's trials before offering them up for assault again that night.

I watch *Angel* at Spice in Noida, a multiplex that seems to bravely provide space to pretty much every murky film released in the National Capital Region that no one else is willing to take up. The thing I like about this place though is that not once in the entire year does a manager bully or emotionally blackmail me into buying two tickets for one film or refuse to run a scheduled show simply because not enough people have turned up to watch it. Over 12 months of unsavoury experiences, a question naturally occurs to me: why do theatre owners accept films that they consider hopeless cases? The answer is manifold. Sometimes they're doing a favour to someone in the financier-producer-distributor chain. Sometimes they're coerced into taking the film, as one multiplex manager explained to me: 'The distributor of Film X is also distributing Film Y. I'm sure Y will be huge, but if I don't take X from him now, then he won't give me Y either, so I'm helpless.' On one occasion, after a couple of untoward incidents at other theatres, I had tracked down Spice's then manager Amit's cellphone number and called him to confirm that he would indeed be running a show of a particular film that was slotted for that evening in newspaper listings. I wanted to guard against driving all the way to discover that it was being cancelled because I was the only one there. 'Don't worry Ma'am,' said the pleasant voice on the phone. 'If it's on our scheduled programme, we will run it, whether only one person or an entire hall full of people turn up.' Nice to know that even a lone customer counts. Good man!

So I return to *Angel*... I'm angry, very angry, as I watch this film alone in a hall with an usher, a curious popcorn seller and another attendant for company. *Angel* is about a boy who falls in love with a physically and mentally challenged girl, and society's reaction to their unconventional relationship. Well, at least I'd imagine that's the concept that choreographer-turned-director Ganesh Acharya had in mind when he started out. What he's ended up making though is a distasteful, muddled-up film in which several bad actors and the overall poor production quality add to the lack of finesse in the treatment of a delicate subject.

The film's pre-release publicity has repeatedly informed us that leading man Nilesh Sahay is Sanjay Dutt's nephew. After watching his performance, I'm afraid I have no sympathy for him. I do however wonder about the heroine, a pretty girl called Maddalsa Sharma who seems to have worked really hard for her role as a woman with a disability in *Angel*. For the second time in the same day, Dylan is ringing in my ears...

I may as well ask her directly. So I track down Maddalsa who, the Internet helpfully informs me, has already starred in a handful of south Indian films. *Angel* is her Hindi debut. When I speak to her, she confirms that she has been acting for three years, since the age of 18. I confess that I don't get opportunities to routinely watch films in Indian languages other than Hindi so I have not seen the films listed in the CV she obligingly e-mails me: director EVV Satyanarayana's *Fitting Master* (Telugu), Sadhu Kokila's *Shaurya* (Kannada) with Darshan, *Alasyam Amrutham* produced by the legendary D Ramanaidu (Telugu) and *Mem Vayasuku Vacham*, also in Telugu.

Okay...so 'what's a sweetheart like you doin' in a dump like *[Angel]*?' Maddalsa Sharma's bio is a fine illustration of the fact that sometimes even talented children from entertainment industry families have to struggle in Bollywood if they're not the offspring of the industry's top-league producers, directors or actors. I mean, if I tell you that her father is producer Subhash Sharma, the name is unlikely to ring a bell with regular Hindi film viewers. Her mother is actress Sheela Sharma née David, a face familiar to today's TV serial viewers though perhaps her calling card to the nation-at-large would be the role of Devaki in BR Chopra's iconic tele-*Mahabharat* of the 1980s.

Maddalsa is a bubbly creature, unfazed by my questions about *Angel*, and chirpy despite her struggles in Bollywood. She explains in detail that directors Abbas-Mustan had offered to launch her when she was in Class 10, but since that project was delayed by about three years, she got restless and took a shot at south Indian cinema. She chatters away so innocently that I don't cut in even at the politically incorrect references to the industries she is currently working in. 'They (Abbas-Mustan) told me, if you don't want to wait and sit idle, you might as well do a south, because south anyway you gain experience. See, as much as you are working and you get to see yourself on screen, you get to know so many things, how camera angles are, how people shoot, what the atmosphere on the sets is, because for a newcomer it's very important to know all these small small details. When you are doing a Bollywood film, you have to be bang on. You have to be perfect. You can't make mistakes. So for that you have to have that little bit of experience, that training period. So I thought I might as well do a south film and get myself polished, and whenever the Hindi film happens, I'll be ready.'

I'm more amused than offended on behalf of south India. So 'south cinema' is a mere training ground for the real thing which is Bollywood? I suspect those remarks would not be pleasing to the ears of her 'south' viewers, but I hold my peace. And any non-'south' person reading this who feels inclined to call me fussy or overly touchy...do ask yourself this question: How do you think we in India would feel if Freida Pinto were to tell the American press that she wanted to do a Hindi film as 'training' for Hollywood because in

Hollywood 'you have to be bang on. You have to be perfect. You can't make mistakes'?

As you may have guessed, one 'south film' led to another and then another for Maddalsa, but she had still not lost sight of her goal: Hindi cinema. When Ganesh Acharya offered her *Angel,* she accepted it because she 'fell in love with the subject'. I can imagine that a skeletal description of the film's story would be impressive. Even though *Angel* infuriated me, I have no doubt either that Acharya meant well.

That said, it's completely unacceptable for a film to feature a doctor saying in passing that the heroine suffers from 'brain trauma injury' without bothering to help the viewer understand what that means. It's equally irresponsible to show the hero indulging in sexual intercourse with this severely disabled girl, without delving into the moral and ethical issues involved. Don't get me wrong. I'm not expecting a feature film to be a documentary on 'brain trauma injury' which a doctor friend has subsequently explained to me. But then, *Rain Man, A Beautiful Mind* or for that matter, India's very own and recent *Taare Zameen Par* and *My Name Is Khan* were not documentaries, but at least they made an effort to be insightful.

Perhaps I should quote a passage from the review I filed on my blog, right after watching *Angel*:

> In the midst of all this is Maddalsa Sharma playing Sonal and trying bravely to make some sense of this nonsense. In places I could actually visualise the director telling her, '*Sridevi ko* Sadma *main dekha hai na? Uss type ka* performance *chahiye. Jaake phir se* DVD *dekho.*' (Have you watched Sridevi in the film *Sadma*? I want that sort

> of performance. Go and watch the DVD again.) It's also weird that the film says Sonal suffers from 'brain trauma injury' while the actress herself has said in an interview that her research for the role included hospital visits to observe patients of cerebral palsy. Did someone tell her they're the same thing?! Still, given the probable ambiguity of the brief and the tackiness of the rest of the proceedings, hers is a performance I won't ignore...

Months later, when I speak to Maddalsa, she explains that she 'worked so hard' on *Angel* 'because the character is suffering from cerebral palsy and audiences are so sharp these days that if you do rubbish they think, *kya ulloo bana rahi hai yeh*' [she's trying to make fools of us]. You have to be absolutely correct. I used to go to Nanavati Hospital [in Mumbai], record those patients on my camera, come home and watch them, try to get their mannerisms and their body language. I did that for almost a month every day, *bahut mehnat karti thi* [I used to work very hard]. Dr Ali Irani of Nanavati Hospital explained things to me in detail, showed me videos. Then I read up a lot on the Net. When I saw the film, I had the satisfaction that my work was good. Whether people liked the film or not, they appreciated my work. Commercially if the film does not do well, it's either the director or producer's fault. The actor is never to be blamed for that but I felt satisfaction that I had done well in my first [Hindi] film,' says the artless 21 year old.

If Ganesh Acharya told her she's a patient of cerebral palsy in *Angel*, did she notice that there is no mention of cerebral palsy in the film? 'There isn't?' No, there isn't. At one point in the film a doctor says she's suffering from brain trauma injury though... 'Brain trauma, *haan haan haan*. Even I noticed that. But in interviews and all, Ganeshji used to openly say she was suffering from cerebral palsy.' Does she recall the words 'cerebral palsy' used in any dialogue in the film? 'No.' Did she wonder why? 'I'm wondering *now*. How many things can we actors think of? But yes, being a director, Ganeshji should have thought of this. You know, Ganeshji is the best choreographer in the business, but direction *sab ke bas ki baat nahin hai* [direction is not everyone's cup of tea]. To translate your vision into an entire film is not easy. Ganeshji narrated the subject so beautifully, but this is an extremely sensitive subject and not everybody could pull it off. I'm too small a person to say this but perhaps Ganeshji does not have the level of experience and maturity for a sensitive subject like this.'

I try to speak to Ganeshji – choreographer for numerous notable Bollywood films – but I give up after a month of being fobbed off by his assistant. As a viewer I cannot condone an actress' failure to notice such a gaping loophole in her film, but at least Maddalsa worked hard on the brief given to her, and fortunately has learnt her lessons from this experience. Having burnt her fingers with *Angel,* this talented girl admits she will be far more cautious when she chooses her next Hindi film. She says: 'I know *na* I have the potential so I don't want to waste myself.' Please don't.

A decade back, you could have said that Maddalsa Sharma does not stand a chance in hell in Bollywood any more. But with all its flaws, this industry does give second leases of life to actresses. Look no further than Genelia D'Souza's return to Bollywood with *Jaane Tu Ya Jaane Na* for an example. If you make the right moves and remain persistent, you could possibly overcome the hurdles of a false start, early mistakes, or a supporting role in a high-profile film though your goal is the heroine slot.

For that last one, I at least will be tracking Swara Bhaskar's career closely. Not 'Swara Who?' any more, but Swara Bhaskar Who Played Kangna Ranaut's Closest Pal in *Tanu Weds Manu*, and Swara whose chocolate-and-caramel-wrapped vocal chords remind me of Priyanka Chopra's voice. Her screen presence was noticeable even in the very drab *Madholal Keep Walking* with which she made her debut in 2010 on the sidelines of Bollywood. And every single *TWM* review that I read takes specific note of her.

About a decade back, I remember Nandita Das mentioning that Ashutosh Gowariker told her she looked 'too intelligent' for Gracy Singh's role in *Lagaan*. Swara looks strikingly intelligent too, but I expect that's no longer an insurmountable hurdle for a female Bollywood aspirant. When she recounts her qualifications to me, it's different from the usual 'modelling experience/beauty pageant victory, acting course, dance classes, gym sessions' routine that I'm used to hearing as a journalist. Nothing particularly wrong with that drill, but it's worth mentioning that Swara is unusual. She is already past her mid-20s in an industry where the top bracket is filled with heroines launched in their teens or early 20s. She is an English (Honours) graduate from Delhi University's Miranda House and holds a Master's degree in Sociology from Jawaharlal Nehru University. She has trained in Bharata Natyam under the renowned dancer Leela Samson. And she has some experience in theatre with JNU's chapter of IPTA (the Indian People's Theatre Association) and NK Sharma's Act One. Now her goal is to be a leading lady in Hindi films.

When I bring up the subject of her one-scene-and-a-few-seconds appearance in *Chillar Party*, she points out that she did it as a favour to a friend on the *Chillar* casting team and discusses the need to be careful in the future because 'I don't want the larger part of my body of work to be one-scene roles, you know with all due respect to anyone who does any kind of work. It's just that for me there's a risk involved because I don't come from a *filmi* background, from a place where there's a *filmi* godfather whose hand is on my head. For someone like me, it's always very easy to get pushed into that space of character work and I don't want to head that way at all, so I'm willing to wait. I needed *Tanu Weds Manu* when it came out. I'm very fortunate to have worked on it because it has done wonders for me but now I'm very clear in my mind that I want substantial lead roles. I've waited for them, and that's what I'm doing now in whatever I'm working on.'

Swara's filmography may be fuller by the time you read this book, but her ambitions don't necessarily mirror the plans of the heterogeneous mix of actors in this chapter. Rajeev Khandelwal, her senior by a decade, is carving his own path in Bollywood. The former cast member of the hit Balaji soap *Kahiin To Hoga* quit that show when his character's popularity was at its peak, only to pick an unconventional 'thinking' role for his Hindi film debut. When he got critical acclaim for his performance in *Aamir* as an Indian Muslim being blackmailed by a terrorist organisation, he surprised everyone by returning to TV to host *Sach Ka Saamna,* India's version of America's *The Moment of Truth.* He isn't particularly looking for lead roles, just roles with substance.

It's working. In 2011, Rajeev played the hero in *Soundtrack,* a film about a deejay who turns deaf and resurrects his career despite the debilitating disability. The role that earned him eyeballs and accolades though was his supporting performance as an irrationally and perennially enraged Mumbai policeman in debutant director Bejoy Nambiar's *Shaitan* produced by Anurag Kashyap. Rajeev's intensity in the film overshadowed even its young and talented lead cast. He had rejected the offer of *Shaitan* several times when first-timer Bejoy approached him earlier but reconsidered when Anurag came on board, feeling reassured that if nothing else, the film would be made with conviction.

'I want to do films that have a shelf life. I don't want to do films simply because *bahut hype hui aur film ne paisa kama liya* [there was a lot of hype and the film earned money], because it's not necessary that I myself would want to watch such a film again,' says the handsome 36-year-old. 'To my mind, that should be my achievement, that when I take a film off my shelf and watch it five years hence, I'll still be proud of it and know that it contributed to altering the course of Indian cinema. Some of my films may work, some may not, but I will never succumb to formula films. I will go by my instincts and not by formulae. I know tomorrow when you talk about the changing face of Hindi films, you will definitely talk about *Shaitan* and *Aamir,* as you will talk about *Phas Gaye Re Obama* and *A Wednesday.* That's the kind of film I want to be a part of because these films are shifting perceptions. They have been accepted at the box office, they are making money and they are being accepted as good films as well. They are also changing the way films will be made in the future because people can see that a small film also works, that a film with first-timers also works if you have your heart in the right place. I'm glad to be a part of this new direction that Indian cinema is taking.'

While Rajeev's career heads in the direction of his choice, others seem to be allowing the tide to take them where it wills. Now be honest…if you weren't reading this book, would you have known that there was another unofficial *Sholay* remake-of-sorts that emerged from Bollywood after *Ram Gopal Varma ki Aag*? Look how much I'm improving your GK! It was called *Bin Bulaye Baaraati*; it was directed by Chandrakant Singh, the same gentleman who inflicted *Be-Careful* on us; it starred Aftab Shivdasani, The Artist Formerly Known as Nisha Kothari, Om Puri, Rati Agnihotri, Vijay Raaz, Sanjay Mishra, Rajpal Yadav, Gulshan Grover and former soap queen Shweta Tiwari with Mallika Sherawat dancing to an item song that goes '*Munni bhi maani aur Sheela bhi maani, Shalu ke tthumke ki duniya deewani.*' (Both Munni and Sheela agree that the world is crazy about Shalu's moves.)

Here's what I'm thinking as I look back at that loud, crude film that I watched in the middle of a rather intimidatingly loud, crude crowd at a multiplex in Gurgaon... No doubt actors who defy convention have to wage many battles in Bollywood but there's no doubt either that if you share Rajeev's worldview and career plans, there's no time like the present time to be in the Mumbai film industry. What better year to illustrate this point than 2011, when senior actor Vijay Raaz starred in *Delhi Belly* with an ensemble cast of bright youngsters but gathered more kudos than the film's 'star' (I use the word in the conventional sense) Imran Khan who had come to *Delhi Belly* fresh from the stupendous success of 2010's *I Hate Luv Storys*. Vijay's poker-faced response to human excrement pouring out of a jar on to his table instead of the diamonds he was expecting will probably go down in film history as one of the Expressions of the Decade. I'd like to pretend though that I didn't also see him in that ignominious *Bin Bulaye Baaraati* in the same year...but I can't. Damn this New Year resolution! Watching *BBB* and discussing it thereafter with the actor helps me understand the difference between Rajeev's single-minded vision for his future and the rather more lackadaisical approach that the supremely talented Vijay admits to.

When he played the tentwallah PK Dubey in Mira Nair's internationally acclaimed Golden Lion-winning, Golden Globe-nominated *Monsoon Wedding*, Vijay Raaz shot into the limelight. He has somehow not had a career graph to match the visibility that that one film gave him. 'After *Monsoon Wedding*, I started getting regular offers and my bread and butter was taken care of,' he recalls. 'But between then and now, there have been many good films I've done such as *Raghu Romeo* in which I played the lead and *Barah Aana* with Naseeruddin Shah, both of which were not released properly, so people didn't get to see them. The distributors of *Raghu Romeo* felt that releasing the film on the same weekend as *Lakshya* would be a good move because they thought *Lakshya* would do so phenomenally well that people coming to theatres who couldn't get tickets for it would buy tickets for *Raghu Romeo* instead. But *Lakshya* failed miserably and *Raghu Romeo* suffered as a result. So after *Monsoon Wedding, Delhi Belly* is a film that people have actually seen and they've liked my performance.'

I curse Bollywood's obsession with pretty faces and well-muscled torsos as I interview this wonderful actor. But there is another point worth looking at. It's not my contention that any actor, writer or director can guarantee a film's success. After all, even the best-written script could be botched up by an incapable editor or director; even the most well-directed film would struggle to become a hit unless it is released strategically and marketed effectively. As a journalist looking in on the industry from the outside, I do however wonder whether the glaringly obvious demerits of a screenplay don't sound a warning bell to seasoned actors like Vijay. Just as his instincts told him 'it was evident that if *Delhi Belly* was made the way it had been written, it would not be an ordinary film,' did he not sense a problem with *Bin Bulaye Baaraati*'s confused script that began fancying itself to be a *Sholay* remake only halfway through the story? Didn't his antennae go on red alert when Priyanka Kothari was cast as *BBB*'s leading lady? Priyanka – earlier known as Nisha – is Ram Gopal Varma's one-time protégé who played the character modelled on Basanti in that more famous and quite abominable *Sholay* remake *Ram Gopal Varma ki Aag*. With her limited acting skills and the sort of image she has built up, didn't the entire cast of *BBB* not doubt the director and producer's commitment to their project when they decided to rope her in? Vijay expresses helplessness in these matters as an actor, when he replies: 'There are many people who have the money to make films but don't have an understanding of cinema, and there are many people who understand cinema but don't have the money. It's very rare that a person understands cinema and also has the money to make good films and the will to market them.'

It's just as rare to meet an actor who has absolute clarity in his mind about his goals and the confidence to bide his time till the right project comes along. In the half decade since he quit *Kahiin To Hoga* for Bollywood, Rajeev Khandelwal has had only three film releases – *Aamir, Shaitan* and *Soundtrack* – but he appears unperturbed, because of his self-belief. And at 40-something-going-on-18, Prashant Narayanan is so unafraid that he doles out undiplomatic answers by the dozen when I chat with him about life after the first big commercial success of his Bollywood career, director Mohit Suri's *Murder 2*.

On his performance as the serial killer and gruesome rapist Dheeraj Pandey in *Murder 2*: 'All the villains we've had in Hindi films so far have been caricatures. From Gabbar Singh onwards they've all been caricatures which are all excellently done characters. The difference with Dheeraj Pandey is that I've really entered your brains, man!'

On his theatre experience as a member of Delhi's Act One and whether it helped him prepare for life as a film actor: 'I don't think theatre helps any actor except people with a lot of time on their hands who think doing theatre is utilising that time correctly. I don't have time for that. I've done theatre for 10 years and I'm pretty bored of it. It doesn't help you be in front of the camera and all I want to do is be in front of the camera.'

On *Shadows Of Time*, a poignant Bengali language German production in which he acted as a young man who never gets over his childhood relationship with Masha, a girl he met when they were both child labourers: 'A careless and ignorant business agent called Bobby Bedi had the distribution rights for *Shadows Of Time* and he kept it under wraps for I don't know what. It's so frustrating for an actor when a beautiful film is not well marketed.' (The Bobby Bedi under discussion here is the man best known as the producer of *Bandit Queen*.)

Next: 'I don't understand what preparation for a role means. I just follow script instincts. I don't prepare. I try to understand what's been written. I'm not into method acting and body building and all these stupid preparations. I just go do my stuff and go home, have a drink.'

Next: 'If I were offered films like *Dabangg, Wanted* and *Ready,* I would not only do them, I'd do a much better job.'

He makes Kareena Kapoor sound tactful, does he not? This is my first ever interview with Prashant and I find myself highly entertained. Through this year of my tiresome resolution, having seen him deliver fine performances in three films (Sudhir Mishra's *Yeh Saali Zindagi, Bhindi Baazaar Inc* and *Murder 2*), I'm also just so grateful to him for those three bright sparks in my largely dreary year that I'm in no mood to judge him.

Prashant has been a consistent performer ever since he made his film debut in the 1990s, but with Dheeraj Pandey he has clocked in his first big role in a big commercial film that went on to become a big hit. Nothing, however, demonstrates the changing face of Bollywood better than the fact that

Emraan Hashmi was keen on playing the murderous Dheeraj Pandey instead of the policeman's role that ultimately went to him in *Murder* 2. The mind rewinds to the knowledge that Amitabh Bachchan had wanted to play Gabbar Singh in *Sholay*, but ended up as Jai. That was in the 1970s. Through the decades, mainstream Bollywood actors all the way from Bachchan till the early 2000s have pretty much conformed to the conventional hero or villain prototypes. In the early part of his career, Shah Rukh Khan dared to risk out-and-out negative-characters-who-didn't-'get-the-girl' in *Baazigar* and *Darr*, and cemented his position in Bollywood. He was an exception. After all these years, it's interesting to discover that Hindi cinema's serial kisser was keen to risk playing a bizarre, eccentric, over-the-top serial killer with no redeeming qualities whatsoever in *Murder* 2.

It's not that the struggle is over for actors like Prashant Narayanan but today's Bollywood does offer them greater opportunities in commercial films than previous decades. It's the sort of scenario that bestows patience on actor Chandan Roy Sanyal *(Kaminey, F.A.L.T.U.)* whose first Bollywood role was as Batukeshwar Dutt in Rakeysh Omprakash Mehra's *Rang De Basanti* for which, he recalls bitterly, he shot for almost two months but found himself reduced to a blink-and-you'll-miss-it appearance in the final product. Before landing in Bollywood, Chandan worked with theatre legend Habib Tanvir in Bhopal and even toured the world with Tim Supple's multi-cultural, multi-lingual *A Midsummer Night's Dream* in which he played a Bengali-and-English-speaking Lysander. Today he juggles ads with Hindi and Bengali film roles only to 'lose all that money' in his theatre group Proscenium in Mumbai. We can't be sure just yet but the commercial success of *F.A.L.T.U.* – in which he was given as much screen time as the producer's son Jackky Bhagnani – could possibly change all that. 'It's very hard to keep your integrity, honesty and sincerity intact, still do good work yet earn enough to make ends meet. It's become more difficult for me to sustain myself,' says Chandan, but then adds just minutes later, 'Irrfan Khan is my role model because he has made his own road in films. I look at him and feel that there's hope for regular Joes like me... The way films are going these days, I'm gonna be someone to reckon with because of the change in cinema which will require actors and scripts.'

Chandan's Bollywood is also home to Oriya actor Pitobash a.k.a. *Shor in the City*'s Mandook and *I Am Kalam*'s Laptan. Before taking off for the Film and Television Institute of India in Pune, Pitobash armed himself with an engineering degree to reassure his middle-class parents 'that I do have something to fall back on, that I am capable of things other than acting too'. Of course they need their Plan Bs in a still-star-struck Bollywood, but that's not stopping these actors from taking risks in films they believe in. Arjun Mathur is a regular in television commercials – remember him in the Airtel 3G ad where he plays a soldier phoning his wife from a remote mountainous location? That cute face is an ad magnet, but films are his professional mainstay. He believes he'd be very good at playing the conventional Hindi film hero, dancing with the heroine and bashing up the villain, but that didn't stop him from kissing a man in Onir's *I Am* in which he stepped into the role of a gigolo. Arjun's wife in the Airtel ad was played by Aditi Rao Hydari who was Sonam Kapoor's Rama Bua in 2009's *Delhi 6* and the gangster's sexually explosive wife in *Yeh Saali Zindagi* (2011). In 2012 she appeared in her first role as a mainstream Hindi film heroine in *London Paris New York*. Aditi's gangster husband in *Yeh Saali Zindagi* was played by Arunoday Singh, grandson of politician Arjun Singh, whose bio-data includes being a nightclub bouncer in New York City 'because actors need experience. The next time someone asks you to play a tough guy and you don't know what it's like to be in a fight, or throw someone out of a brawl, what will you do?'

Arunoday adds: "When I told my family my career plans, my parents giggled and my sisters doubled up with laughter because they found it hilarious that the shyest guy there ever was wanted to be an actor. I used to be pathologically shy. But that's an advantage for an actor because quiet people watch more, notice more, have more energy, and when quiet people get up on stage, they explode.' If you've witnessed the spontaneous combustion occurring each time he and Aditi appeared together in a single shot in *Yeh Saali Zindagi*, you would be inclined to agree.

These are actors with patience and self-confidence, making their own road in the film industry against seemingly – but not entirely – unbeatable odds. It's impossible not to notice them even in small supporting roles. It's hard not to root for them when they get to play the lead. It also really requires all your strength not to deride Bollywood – yes even this gradually changing Bollywood – for taking it's time to give them the space they deserve. I had tears of laughter in my eyes as I watched the ultra-Punjabi, Caneda-crazed Poli in the 2011 Dharmendra-Sunny-Bobby-starrer *Yamla Pagla Deewana* telling Bobby's character

Gajodhar: '*Tussi bade* impotent *ho ji.*' (You are very impotent.) Umm...to those of you not familiar with Punjabi accents, Poli intended to say 'important'. Actress Sucheta Khanna who plays Poli was to have been launched as a Hindi film heroine over a decade back in Amitabh Bachchan Corporation Limited's *Naam Kya Hai* co-starring a young Mukul Dev. Fate and ABCL's bankruptcy intervened, so she moved on to a television career with a string of shows including *Comedy Circus 2* and *Lapataganj*. Now the acclaim for *YPD* has led to *YPD 2* and who knows where the future will take her. Sucheta is happy at the way her career has turned out though, and is determined 'not to take up filler roles in films as some people do, simply to prove that I'm doing films'. Wise girl, but anyone who enjoys good acting would be hoping that Bollywood has the good sense to offer her more with each passing year. Fingers crossed too for the much younger Kriti Malhotra who played the girl in the home videos that fall into Arun/Aamir Khan's hands in *Dhobi Ghat*; for senior theatre actor Rajesh Sharma who played the corrupt-yet-good-at-heart policeman and Sabrina Lal's ally in *No One Killed Jessica* (*NOKJ*) and producer Selva Ganesh who discovers Silk in *The Dirty Picture*; and for Sharma's co-star Neil Bhoopalam who played Vikram Jai Singh, the witness who turns hostile in *NOKJ*, delivering this memorable line, 'If you were given a choice between a crore of rupees and a bullet, what would you choose? I don't want a crore, but I don't want a bullet either.'

And if you're reading this, Bollywood, instead of casting random white folk in ancillary roles, would you mind noting down the names Emma Brown Garrett and Beatrice Ordeix? Emma is the Australian actress now based in Mumbai who played Sunny Deol's English-Hindi-and-Punjabi-spewing *gori* wife in *YPD*. And Ordeix is a Delhi-based French actress who you may have seen as the benevolent foreigner Gulshan Grover falls in love with in *I Am Kalam*. Unlike the white policemen in *Kites* and *Kurbaan*, THESE GIRLS CAN ACT!!!

As I run through the 121 films big and small that I've seen for this book, I realise that I'd need more space than my publishers have given me to introduce you to every talented actor I've seen waiting in the wings, many for much longer than they ought to have considering the immense talent they bring to the table. Did I mention Radhika Apte from *Shor in the City* and *I Am*? Or Girija Oak from *Shor in the City* and a dreary Subhash Ghai production called *Cycle Kick* that I bet 99.999 per cent of you have not even heard of? I want so much to introduce you to the attractive Tamil-Telugu actor Sundeep Kishan who made his Hindi debut with *Shor in the City*; Nikhil Dwivedi whose debut in a poorly made film called *My Name Is Anthony Gonsalves* in 2008 belies the talent that was so much in evidence in Mani Ratnam's *Raavan* (2010) in which he was the modern-day Lakshman of the story and *Shor in the City*; Deepak Dobriyal of *Tanu Weds Manu* who really deserves better than 2011's *Teen Thay Bhai* in which he co-starred with Om Puri and Shreyas Talpade; Abhimanyu Singh who plays the chillingly homophobic policeman in *I Am* and...and...and... Oh, I can go on! It's easy to be frustrated because life and Bollywood do not always move at the pace a film buff might hope for. Today, more than ever though, it's a good time to be optimistic about this industry that still short changes talent too often because it's accompanied by a face that fails to fall within its conventional definition of pretty/handsome, or does not bring to the table a 'fair' complexion, dancing skills, family connections and/or the willingness to be formulaic.

It's optimism after all that has prompted Poorna Jagannathan – the attractive Tunisia-born, US-based actress of Indian origin – to set up a second home in Mumbai and give Bollywood a serious shot. Poorna does not possess the regular light-skinned face that mainstream Bollywood still seems to favour for its leading ladies. To those who've seen her play Imran Khan's buddy/colleague/lover in *Delhi Belly* though, it's clear that she has oodles of pizzazz and sex appeal. Not being a Xerox copy of her contemporaries is probably what made her stand out in the eyes of a Hindi film audience increasingly demanding the offbeat and accepting the avant-garde even from mainstream filmmakers. So firm is Poorna's faith in the opportunities this changing scenario offers, that she has decided to shuttle between Mumbai and Los Angeles, despite a recurring role in the US television series *Royal Pains*. That's a lot of trouble to put yourself through to 'stay relevant in both places.' Does she think she fits the conventional image of a Hindi film heroine? 'You know the answer to that as well as I do,' Poorna replies. 'I'm the antithesis of the conventional heroine but I don't think that's a bad thing. I think the market is changing faster than we think. People are ready for unconventional choices in scripts and talent.'

True enough. And the people who embraced a wiry-haired Poorna in *Delhi Belly* and fell in love once again with Vijay Raaz in the same film, see the heroine's best friend in *Tanu Weds Manu* (*TWM*) and wonder when they'll see her as a leading lady.

XYZ PRODUCTIONS PRESENTS
?
new in theatres

As I emerge from the theatre after watching *TWM*, I spot a standee in the lobby giving me a group shot of Tanu's and Manu's families, friends and *baraatis*. Kangna Ranaut (heroine) – check; R Madhavan (hero) – check; Deepak Dobriyal (hero's best friend) – check; Eijaz Khan (heroine's best friend's fiancé, also an interesting and handsome actor) – check; Swara Bhaskar (heroine's best friend) – hold on... I do a double take. Where is Ms Bhaskar in that lot? The lady herself refuses to comment on the question. And Viacom 18's then development and creative head Anku Pande is embarrassed when I phone to ask her about this oversight. 'It's just one of those things, schedules not matching or something like that,' she says. 'And let's face it, you realise how lovely Swara is only after you see the film, but her picture on a poster was not exactly going to draw audiences into the hall in the first place. For that we needed Maddy and Kangna.' But, I persist, I'm not disputing the posters featuring only Maddy and Kangna; I'm referring to the group shot with all the actors playing Tanu, Manu, their relatives and friends. Why was everyone except Swara in that picture? Anku laughs uncomfortably and says, 'Maybe you need to talk to my marketing team.' I decide not to, because I realise that I'm unlikely to ever be told the absolute truth about this omission. Who knows what practical issues or politics, rivalries or warped logic come into play when a film is being marketed?

I do bring it up in a conversation with Swara though. 'I didn't ask why I was excluded from the posters because I don't want to,' she replies. 'What will stay forever is the film. As an actor, one is prone to insecurity but your work will speak for itself. So yes, I'm not on the posters of *Tanu Weds Manu*, but all these months later you are calling me, right?' Right.

8

The Unbearable Sadness of Being a Filmaniac

Every silver lining has a cloud. This book has brought me in touch with some gorgeous talents that may now be floundering in the wilderness but will hopefully grab the spotlight some day. It has reminded me of the new face of Bollywood that is increasingly seeking out such gifted people. Many of them may still not have got the centre stage they deserve, yet the situation is getting better for at least some of them. Not enough has changed; a lot certainly has.

A year of watching the teeniest films produced by the industry has also brought along its share of heartbreak. I can cope with seeing a talented actor starring in rubbish to survive. There's nothing more distressing though than encountering a superstar who does not seem to care any more…or a legend who has lost touch with the world.

February 10

It is after watching *Tum Hi To Ho* with Vipinno that a feeling of melancholy seeps into this journey that I embarked upon in January. You remember the film? I told you about it… You know that outrageously awful one starring the businessman from Mozambique? As Vipinno's Rajiv goes on a murderous spree in *Tum Hi To Ho,* a detective enters the picture. He's a handsome fellow, tall and well built, with a proud moustache teasing his upper lip, a twinkle lurking around the corners of his eyes. He seems strangely out of place though in this temple to mediocrity, and completely uninvolved.

February 22

I see him again, lumbering across the screen with not a care in the world, in a lacklustre children's film called *Satrangee Parachute,* in a role so small that I can barely recall it.

June 16

Bhindi Baazaar Inc is a rather well-acted, well-produced gangster flick about underworld rivalries on the streets of Mumbai. It lacks novelty no doubt, but it's certainly not a film that anyone associated with it should be ashamed of. What is HE doing here though, randomly popping up without an explanation and then wandering off wordlessly in more than one scene? I assure you, I'm not exaggerating. That's a very precise description of his role in the film. What does it mean?

August 29

Now here he is in Pammi Somal's *Mummy Punjabi,* playing a man who has harboured a life-long crush on Kirron Kher's boisterous Punjaban from whom the film derives its title. Despite the inconsistent screenplay and characterisation, Kirron braves her way through this flawed film with her spirited performance. You watch her transition from the energetic middle-aged woman of the first half of the film to the broken and lonely soul she later becomes, and you know she deserves so much better in this godforsaken industry that can't see beyond bikini-enabled 20- and 30-somethings. There *he* is though, looking inexplicably detached despite the significance and length of his role in the film. It's as if he's not even trying.

October 6

By the time I chance upon him yet again in Dev Anand's last film *Chargesheet*, I know I have to meet this man and ask, why?! Having witnessed such glory and stardom, why would he blot his CV in inconsequential or poorly sketched roles or worse, in films so terrible that when I first phone him for an interview for this book, he asks softly, 'You've been around for a while so you *do* know I've done films other than the ones you've mentioned, don't you?'

Of course I know! For Chrissake, you are Jackie Shroff!! Why are you doing this to yourself and to all those fans who invested their time, money and energy in your films?!!!

Such screaming emotions are reserved for the confines of my mind, of course. I am more composed when I finally meet Shroff late one evening at his friend's farmhouse in one of Delhi's most moneyed and secluded localities. Since he reigned in Bollywood before I became a journalist, this is my first meeting with this superstar of the 1980s. Back then, he was seen as a possible successor to Amitabh Bachchan along with Anil Kapoor,

Mithun Chakraborty, Sanjay Dutt and Sunny Deol. His roles in landmarks of that decade such as *Hero, Ram Lakhan, Parinda* and *Tridev* established him as a good-looking guy who could command crowds and also act. But unlike his friend, rival and contemporary Anil Kapoor whose fitness and longevity are now part of Bollywood folklore, and whose persistence has led to a second career on the international stage since *Slumdog Millionaire,* Shroff has virtually dropped out of sight.

When I arrive for our interview, he is friendly, warm and solicitous. Was it tough locating this house? What could he offer me to drink? Would I rather not move closer to the *angeetthi* since it's so cold out here on the lawn?

Oh no, I think to myself, if he'd been boorish and standoffish, this would've been so much easier. But a job's a job, so I let out an inward sigh and begin our Q&A: What are the criteria based on which he chooses his films? 'Some films I do for a lark, some because I like the director, some because the production house is good like *Anna Bond,* a Kannada film I've done under Dr Rajkumar's banner...,' he counts the conditions off his fingers.

Then why did he act in *Tum Hi To Ho?*

This is the most unusual interview I've ever had with a film star. Shroff does not remember the film! I remind him of Vipinno, of how *Tum Hi To Ho* was promoted as the first Bollywood film to star a hero from Africa. When I describe his role as a detective, a look of recognition flickers across his face. 'Oh Lord, that director was an assistant director somewhere in one of the 150 or so films I've done! He said, "*Yaar please kar. Tu karega toh mere ko picture milega.*" [Please do it. If you agree to do this role, I'll get the film.] Like that, a lot of assistant directors come to me saying, "*Yaar yeh kar de to mera production shuru ho jayega, main kaam shuru kar sakta hoon.*" [If you do this, my production will start, I can start work.] I say, "Are you sure *mere karne se teri zindagi ban jayegi? Toh bana.*" [Are you sure if I do this role your life would be made? Then make it.] It never bothered me. Friends have told me not to do these things but I don't think too much.'

Satrangee Parachute?

'*Haan, bachchon ki picture. Toh bachchon ke liye kiya. Kuchh bhi nahin socha.*' (It was a children's film, so I did it for the children. Didn't stop to think about it.)

And that cameo in *Bhindi Baazaar Inc*...what did it mean?

'You know how the story was being narrated in flashback by those two men playing chess. So I think I was supposed to be a pawn. *Kuchh socha nahin, jo bola woh kiya.*' (I didn't give it any thought, just did as I was told.)

I wonder if a person who has scaled such heights should not be more careful in his choice of roles and films. You are, after all, Jackie Shroff! '*Baahar jaate hai toh maaloom padta hai. Bachche se leke, security, bathroom sambhaalne waale se lekar air hostess, sab photo lete hai.*' (When I step out you will witness my stardom. Children, security staff, bathroom cleaners, airhostesses – they all line up to take photographs.)

But you've done so many big films and big roles. Aren't you spoiling your filmography now? '*Na na na. Kya farak padta hai, dost? Main toh abhi bhi jaata hoon toh poora plane ek side pe tilt ho jaata hai* where I sit.' (No no no. What difference does it make, my friend? Even today when I travel, the entire plane tilts towards the side where I sit.)

By now I'm torn between actually enjoying this interview and being distraught about his don't-care attitude! It seems there's nothing I can ask this man that could get him ruffled as we sit there warming ourselves by the smouldering coals on this cold Delhi night. Many weeks later, when I recount this conversation to veteran journalist Rauf Ahmed, he's not surprised. He recalls instead one morning in Mumbai in 1983, when *Hero* – young Jackie Shroff's first film as a leading man – was released. Rauf, who was the editor of *Movie* magazine at the time, says: 'Jackie's the first guy I saw in my entire career who was sleeping on the first day of the launch of his film. I had seen *Hero* the film 3-4 days before its release at a trial show and I felt that this guy would be a star who would overtake his contemporaries like Anil Kapoor. So I had decided to put him on the magazine cover. I had told him I would be coming over for an interview with Vir Sanghvi, but when we got to his house he was fast asleep. I couldn't believe it. Here the whole industry was watching because he was a newcomer in a Subhash Ghai film, and Ghai had replaced Sanjay Dutt in *Hero* because Sanjay had given him a lot of trouble in *Vidhaata*. I asked Jackie, "Don't you want to know how people have received your film?" and he said, "No, what difference does it make whether I know?" In that sense, he was very philosophical. Some of his contemporaries would have been jumping around talking about the film to the whole world, but not Jackie. He never lobbied for media coverage or awards. He had tremendous faith in his father who was an astrologer. And his father had told him that this film cannot go wrong, that for the next 15 years or so he could move on blindly and nothing would go wrong with him.

True enough, till 1997-98 he was going great guns. By 2000, Jackie felt he had overstayed in Bollywood because he used to tell me, "My father said I would be here till 1997-98". Perhaps other things went wrong too, I don't know, but by then he had lost his drive.'

Let me not digress though. Let me steer you back to my own first encounter with Jackie Shroff, in Delhi about three decades after *Hero* made him a star. Shroff is waving aside my worries about *Tum Hi To Ho* and *Satrangee Parachute*. He asks me to note instead that he was the one who started the trend of leading men doing negative roles. He describes himself as a hippie and is tickled when I ask if he is not concerned about finances. He seems satisfied collaborating with the Union Ministry of Railways on a railway safety programme that he tells me is at a nascent stage, doing some social work, indulging in a spot of organic farming, cooking, considering a proposal to start an acting school, being a dad...

Yet, this is a man who clearly has a lot of acting left in him. At 55, he is pleased as can be about the positive reviews he has garnered for his role as a don on the decline in the 2011 Tamil film *Aaranya Kaandam* which picked up two National Awards in early 2012. Now *there's* a film worthy of his talent and track record. *Aaranya Kaandam* features Shroff as an ageing gangster struggling to cope with sexual impotence, a young mistress who feels repelled by him and a one-time protégé in rebellious mode. Shroff is understated in this film yet manages to underline his character's eccentricity and frustration. It is an act that would have his fans rewinding to Vidhu Vinod Chopra's seminal underworld film *Parinda* in 1989, in which Shroff delivered an award-winning performance as a man driven to crime by circumstance but torn between his profession and love for his honest younger brother (Anil Kapoor).

The country's film-viewing habits being the way they are though, few regular Hindi film-goers are aware of the existence of the Tamil *Aaranya Kaandam*. To them, Shroff is a star who fell by the wayside, a man whose time is past. As I interview him, I find him entirely unmoved by nostalgia for his career highs. The only time the calm demeanour is even marginally tousled is when I ask if he does not miss doing leading roles in Hindi films of the sort that Amitabh Bachchan still gets while being in the vicinity of 70, and Anil Kapoor continues to attract in his 50s? 'Anil is *toh* evergreen, but that two-bit role in *MI4*. What was that role?'

I'm talking about Anil's roles in Hindi films not Hollywood, I point out. 'Ya but *abhi baat kar rahey hai toh* [since we are on the subject], he is doing that kind of thing. You know you do anything that hits your heart. I didn't even think about these things when I did *Khalnayak*, *Parinda* or *Mission Kashmir*. *Mujhe bola gaya ki saat scene hai Jaggu, karega?* [I was told, there are seven scenes Jaggu, will you do it?] But I knew that irrespective of how much screen time I got, the scenes would be so strong, that I'd be the one everyone remembers. The role of Chunnilal that I did in *Devdas* was rejected by so many actors but it didn't matter to me. Because after the film, everyone was talking like Chunni Babu, not like Devdas – they would come up to me and say *yaar ch se chai le aa, d se dil, d se duniya*, they were talking like that. So it's not the length, it's the strength, whether it's seven or two scenes. Even in *Bhindi Baazaar* I had

only two scenes but everyone was saying, "Jaggu, *kya kaam kiya*!" (What a performance!) Erm…if you say so, Jaggu Dada.

He happily mimics Dev Anand while telling me how the legend had advised him never to have regrets. He slips into his best Bambaiyya accent as he expounds his philosophy of life: '*Bindaas rehne ka,* tension *lene ka nahin.*' (Chill, relax, don't be tense.) And when I ask if he looks back at the days of *Ram Lakhan* et al, he chuckles softly as he says: 'Humpty Dumpty sat on a wall, Humpty Dumpty had a great fall. All the king's horses and all the king's men, couldn't you know, *ud gaya toh ud gaya* [what's over is over]. Live for now.'

It's getting late and I have a long drive back home. We chat as he walks me to my car describing his forthcoming films. Perhaps he senses my schizophrenic reaction to this interview. I don't know…but as I wave goodbye, he goes Bambaiyya on me again and calls out: 'Tension *nahin lene ka, bidu.*'

Okay…*bidu*.

~

The evening with Jackie Shroff takes my mind back to an earlier encounter with Dev Anand…this one on screen though. 12.20 pm: I've arrived 15 minutes early at PVR-MGF Metropolitan Mall to book my ticket for Devsaab's *Chargesheet*. 'Sorry Ma'am, the show's been cancelled,' the attendant at the ticket counter says nonchalantly. Is he kidding me? And why has it been cancelled? 'Because no one has come to watch the show,' he replies coolly. Hello, I'm here. What do you mean 'no one has come'? This guy must be from another planet. He looks at me without batting an eyelid and replies: 'You're late. We can

CHARGE-SHEET:
Running Now....
Dev Anand's
CHARGESHEET

cancel the show if no one buys a ticket by the scheduled time.' I show him my watch, at which point he informs me that my watch is slow and it's actually past 12.35 pm. So I pull out two cellphones from my handbag, wave them back and forth before his glass window and ask: 'Are both these slow too?'

The chap hesitates, leaves his seat to consult a senior, then returns to sell me a ticket. This is just the first hurdle that I face in my quest to watch *Chargesheet*. Perhaps I'm the only patron who has turned up for this film all week. I can think of no other reason why the usher would forget to remove the barricades outside the hall until after the scheduled time, and then too only because I knock at the door. My suspicions are confirmed. The attendant in the hall tells me apologetically that since no one else has come to see this film in six days, he assumed no one would be here today either.

Impressed by my own purposefulness, I settle down in my seat, a modern-day Jhansi *ki* Rani with a notebook, popcorn, coffee and momos spread around me. For the cost of one ticket, it seems like I've got the entire hall to myself…again. It's been many years since I last saw a new Dev Anand production. It occurs to me with a tinge of sorrow, that it's been many years since most of India made the effort to watch a new Dev Anand production. The towering star of 1950s-'70s cinema has been soldiering on in the past three decades, producing, writing, directing and starring in films that no one seems to be watching; scouting for new talent, launching new faces, in spite of the virtually non-existent audience and the critical ridicule or at best silence that his last dozen films have received. I've been reading about Devsaab's many recent celluloid misadventures, but how bad could it possibly be, I wonder? After all, he remained an enchanting interviewee till the very end, a seemingly level-headed man with enviable verve and energy levels. I recall interviewing him myself at the Cannes Film Festival in France in 2008, the year *Guide* was screened in the Cannes Classics section. He was a joy to talk to, full of beans and plans, thrilled at this late entry into the world's most prestigious film festival. I suspect that Dev Anand's fans from his heyday have consciously remained stuck in a time warp. I suspect too that those who grew up watching his greatest films would be shattered if they were here with me today as *Chargesheet* unspools at this Gurgaon multiplex.

Shhh! Silence! The Navketan logo flashes on screen. Then come the opening scenes of the film that immediately bring me crashing down. The gangster Sultanbhai (Naseeruddin Shah) is in Dubai, gazing down at his moll Maria from a window. As she lies sunbathing below, the camera gives us a glimpse of one nipple through the fabric of her swimsuit. What seems like a lifetime later, Maria is now in a microscopic blouse and hotpants at a police station in India. Never mind the plot. She sits on the floor, her legs spread out, the camera staying determinedly between her thighs. Then at some point (who cares why) she rises to run out of the room but instead of moving with her, the camera stays fixed and she does not run *away* from the camera, she runs *into* it, so that her bouncing bosom gets larger and larger until all we see is her skin. Cut to the next scene.

There is a murder somewhere along the way, and a husband who slaps his wife and shouts, '*Besharam, behaya!*' (You shameless wench!) – I can't remember the last time I heard that outdated dialogue in a Hindi film. A bunch of youngsters who can't act have been cast in various parts. And politician Amar Singh makes one of the worst-acted guest appearances in the history of Bollywood. I can see why Dev Anand would act in this film – after all he's the writer, producer and director of *Chargesheet*. I can sort of see why Jackie Shroff might agree to play a substantial part in this film – after all, having made his debut in a film by Devsaab, he must be beholden to the great man. But why does a stalwart like Naseeruddin Shah sign up for such a low-brow production, then proceed to add insult to the injury caused to his admirers by hamming his way through the film?

Half an hour into *Chargesheet*'s running time, a young couple enters the hall. Another twosome looking for an empty theatre which lends itself to some good ol' necking, I assume, perhaps unfairly. Well, if that was their intention, then it looks like they were startled into watching *Chargesheet* by the compelling content unfolding on screen. The film is so awful that I succumb to fits of hysterical laughter. At some point, my two fellow audience members get up to leave. I'm in a jovial mood so I call out to them: 'Why are you leaving? Aren't you having fun?' The girl replies: 'Are you serious? You're actually enjoying this film? We could hear someone in the hall laughing, but we thought it might be an usher since we didn't see you when we entered.' I laugh. 'It's just one of those films that's so bad that I'm enjoying it,' I say. 'Well, good luck to you,' she signs off. 'We're leaving. We saw the credits and thought it might be nice, but what on earth is this?'

A sobering thought. If you are an infrequent film viewer who does not follow reviews too closely, you too might assume that a film starring Dev Anand, Naseeruddin Shah and Jackie Shroff would be good. Maybe stars do owe something to the members of the public who built them up and gave them their stature. My laughter is now tempered with sadness at the thought of how my octogenarian mother would feel if she were sitting here with me, watching her idol Dev Anand's *Chargesheet*.

My mind darts around that hall, pondering various philosophical questions, succumbing to distress and delight by turns as *Chargesheet* persists unrelentingly on screen. The innocent local girl Chhamchham is batting her heavily shaded eyelids for the nth time on screen and I notice that her makeup artist, who was probably instructed to make her look white skinned for the film, seems to have forgotten to touch up the lower rims of her eyelids. So she's white from head to toe but her lower lids remain dark, contributing some more to my mirth. In a murder scene that might give the makers of *CSI* a serious complex, policemen don't lift fingerprints off surfaces at a crime scene; they only click photographs of spots where there might be prints. The shabbiness of the film is truly heart-wrenching. The fact that it bears Devsaab's name compounds the tragedy of it all.

Maybe the people who were indulging an old man by associating themselves with his films were doing him a disservice. After all, it's up to the youth to help the elderly retain their dignity in their twilight years. Were these so-called friends and well-wishers doing Devsaab any favours by standing by and watching while he made himself a laughing stock among a once-adoring audience and a new generation that had not seen his halcyon days?

There have been rumours for years in Bollywood that Devsaab's later films were financed by an NRI fan, a possible explanation for why he remained a prolific filmmaker till the very end, unconcerned by the financial losses incurred each time. Mohan Churiwala, his long-time associate, denies these rumours vehemently when I ask. 'Devsaab never borrowed a penny from anyone to make his films. He was a wealthy man and he has left his son a very wealthy man too,' Churiwala insists.

What's not in the realm of mere rumour is that *Chargesheet* was distributed by Warner Bros India although Devsaab's track record in the last three decades is well known in film circles. To what end did Warner pick up the film? And having done that, why would an unnamed executive of the company proceed to insult the association with this quote in the press – 'We had no expectations from the movie' – after it bombed?

Arrey! And then comes my experience at this PVR in Gurgaon. I'm still watching as *Chargesheet* draws to a close. The end credits start to roll. Just then the screen goes blank. Excuse me, but I'm still here. I summon the usher, and tell him he needs to visit the projection room and instruct them to run the credits. I get no particular thrill from doing so, but an injustice is an injustice. Besides, if I am to review this film on my blog, I need to note down the names of some cast members since there's no telling whether such a film would have an exhaustive official website. The usher returns. Apparently the projectionist just assumed that there was no one in the hall since no one had come to watch *Chargesheet* all week, and so stopped the film before it was through. 'Then tell him to re-start it,' I say, 'or call your theatre manager. I've bought a ticket and even if I didn't have a job to do, I have a right to watch the film till the very last credit rolls.'

The manager arrives to inquire what happened, apologises in all earnestness, goes off to the projection room where I hear him yelling at someone and the film starts rolling again. If the grand old man had known how *Chargesheet* was being treated, I wonder how he might have felt.

Showing true respect to an artist should not involve humouring and indulging the eccentricities of his old age; it involves protecting him from public scorn. Fortunately for Dev Anand's memory, virtually no one saw *Chargesheet*. The trade website *boxofficeindia.com* reports that the film collected just ₹ 3 lakh at the box office. Assuming the average ticket price was ₹ 150 at theatres where it was released, this means that only approximately 2,000 tickets were sold – NATIONWIDE! Assuming further that a large majority of those who bought tickets to this film were indulging in activities that did not require them to look at the screen, I guess we can safely conclude that hardly a handful of human beings watched this film.

Fortunately for me, just a few months prior to *Chargesheet*'s release, I had re-watched a Dev Anand classic on the big screen. Early in 2011, Navketan had released a colourised version of *Hum Dono*, calling it *Hum Dono Rangeen*. Now *there* was a memory worth reviving – a dashing young Dev Anand in a double role in the 1960s courting the glamorous Sadhana and romancing the very pretty Nanda. It was poorly publicised but that mattered not to the sparse audience at Delite cinema in central Delhi where I saw it. I remember joining them in singing along 'Main zindagi ka saath nibhaata chala gaya' and 'Abhi na jaao chhodkar, ke dil abhi bharaa nahin.'

R.I.P. You Crazy Diamond! R.I.P. Dev Anand – actor, director, producer, legend!

9

And His Father Asked, *'Kaisi Lagi?'*

As my research for this book gallops along, I'm working at a maniacal pace, watching films, then writing, then watching films some more, then writing again. In the midst of the madness, Rohit Khattar calls on behalf of industrialist Anand Mahindra's Mumbai Mantra. They're holding a screenplay workshop for film writers in association with the Sundance Institute founded by Robert Redford, and would I be willing to join the selection committee? Winners get to develop their screenplays at a lab to be conducted by a richly talented panel of film industry stalwarts. Oh noooooo! I'm drowning in work here, but Rohit is the sort of man who asks so politely that it's impossible to say no to him. Besides, if I constantly bombard Bollywood with complaints about poorly written films and their inadequate support to independent filmmakers, declining participation in this pioneering effort seems wrong. More importantly, if you intend to write about films, then it's always a good idea to gather as much knowledge as you can about the backroom operations behind the final celluloid product (the professorial tone of that last sentence makes me smile when I re-read it – blame it on the fact that it's what I tell my journalism students in the classroom since the practice has stood me in good stead in the field). As much as I've learnt from compulsively viewing films, reviewing them, interviewing film personalities and reading up on cinema, I've also learnt a great deal from hanging out on a couple of film sets, reading the occasional screenplay sent to me by a film writer keen on frank feedback, closely observing camerapersons, lighting technicians, makeup artists and other colleagues during my years as a television professional, watching other TV producers and editors at work, scripting and overseeing edits myself in my own role as a TV producer, even learning to do my own makeup, however marginal to the proceedings that may seem to a layperson. So I agree to read a bunch of screenplays for the Sundance workshop, pray that God suddenly decides to bestow 48 hours on each day of my life, and set out to brave the rest of my year.

~

'By my troth, Nerissa, my little body is aweary of this great world.' And by my troth, dear reader (with due apologies to William Shakespeare's Portia), if I had known that I would be meeting politician Ram Vilas Paswan this evening, I would not have carelessly heaved myself into billowing drawstring trousers, an elephantine jacket and floaters before setting off to watch my film previews of the day. By my troth, if I had known he would be here, I would in fact have stayed away.

It turns out that the screening of Paswan's son Chirag Paswan's debut film *Miley Naa Miley Hum* is being held at such a late hour that most of the city's critics who are aware of it don't turn up. I've got an impossibly packed schedule on the day of the film's release so I grit my teeth and attend the preview, not realising that the hall will be largely bereft of journalists and I'll find myself in the midst of an intimate gathering consisting of the hero's family and friends. I sink into my seat and pretend to be fascinated by my cellphone, hoping no one will notice me. But oh dear, the film's publicist did not inform me that the person with whom she is coordinating the arrangements, the friendly boy who has been talking to me on the phone, is not a PR agent – he's Chirag's friend. And Chirag's friend informs Paswan Senior about my presence in the hall.

Mr Paswan walks up to my seat to say hello. It's the sort of situation every critic should avoid. The films we intend to review should be watched in detached settings, not in the company of the hero's sweet elderly father who is attentive to a fault and insists on treating me as his guest. Since I've already told you I avoid discussions with the team of a film before I write my review, you can imagine how awkward I must feel being with the leading man's relatives during the preview.

As *Miley Naa Miley Hum* begins, I'm determined to stay glued to my cellphone during the break to avoid any interaction with Chirag's family. My plan is quickly nixed. When the word 'interval' flashes on screen, and I stick my cell to my ear to make a call, Paswan calls out to me and absolutely insists that I join him for snacks. To say no when he is surrounded by family would be rude beyond belief. What am I to do?!

So I chat with him about Bihar, Jharkhand, Kerala, India's shockingly poor tourism promotions abroad, politics in his home state, anything that comes to mind to avoid questions about the film. My discomfiture is not a comment on the quality of the film. I just happen to sincerely and genuinely believe that I should not be socialising with anyone close to a film that I plan to review. This, however, is a unique situation that I've never found myself in before. The film resumes playing and as soon as the end credits roll, I begin to make a call and walk out of the hall…but Paswan Senior walks up to me and asks: '*Kaisi lagi?*' (How did you find it?)

Many years back, I remember Amarr Upadhyay – best known as Mihir from Ektaa Kapoor's *Kyunki Saas Bhi Kabhi Bahu Thi* – attending the press show in Delhi for his debut Hindi film *Dhund The Fog*. To put it kindly, it was a terrible film! *Miley Naa Miley Hum* is miles ahead of it on the quality barometer! As journalists streamed out of the theatre, Amarr stood there at the door wishing everyone. I was very junior then and at a loss for what to say. So I closely watched my seniors, each of whom seemed to find something appropriate to say to the very evidently apprehensive star, before dashing off. When my turn came, I shook hands with him and said, 'So all the best Amarr,' and ran away.

This is different though. This is not a young star or producer or director or publicist…

Do I tell Chirag's Dad the truth? That the film is not up to the mark? Do I tell him that while I have no issues with his son's performance or screen presence, I do believe his face had been plastered with makeup to embarrassing effect?

Would it make sense to this non-*filmi* man if instead I were to launch into my stock lines about how I don't, as a matter of principle, comment on a film to anyone until I've finished writing my review, and could I request him to please read my blog instead?

My presence of mind betrays me right at that moment as I stare into the face of an anxious father with family and friends all around him, and I smile and say, '*Ji, achchhi lagi*' (Sir, I liked it) before escaping.

I have no idea whether Ram Vilas Paswan visits the blogosphere or whether my review of his son's first film was brought to his attention by the PR agent. I do know with the benefit of hindsight that I should have noiselessly exited that theatre the minute I discovered that the family was in the hall.

Oh well, that's a lesson learnt.

~

And so my year is racing towards its inevitable end. Bollywood is celebrating the unprecedented number of hits it has notched up, Salman seems unstoppable, Shah Rukh is on shaky ground but then swiftly redeems himself, and Vidya Balan has scored a blockbuster in the form of a heroine-centric *masala* entertainer against all odds.

The industry is going through a historic churn. And the thing I enjoy most about this year is how much so many industry insiders enjoy demystifying their business for the benefit of a journalist who's keen to know. During seemingly endless interviews, they gladly offer answers to my every probing question.

It's certainly a scenario worth probing. Eros Group's biggest films in 2009 were the Akshay Kumar-Kareena Kapoor-starrer *Kambakkht Ishq* and *Love Aaj Kal* with Saif Ali Khan, Deepika Padukone and Rishi Kapoor. Both were released on 1,400 screens each across the country. In 2011, their most expansive release was the SRK-starrer *Ra.One* on 3,100 screens!

In December 2009, Reliance Entertainment released the Aamir Khan-R Madhavan-Sharman Joshi-starrer *3 Idiots* on 1,789 screens; in December 2011 the figure for *Don* 2 with Shah Rukh is a comparatively mind-boggling 3,105 screens.

It's the same story with every one of Mumbai's production and distribution majors. The scale of Bollywood's film releases is expanding at a mountainous rate. Kamal Jain, Group CFO-India for Eros, explains to me with painstaking patience and passion the reasoning behind these altered release strategies across the industry. I soak it all in, refer back to my conversations with his industry peers and my own mental notes through my years as a journalist, translate it all from French and Latin, to give you my understanding and interpretation of the facts...

With the rapid increase in the number of entertainment options available to the audience, film companies are unfolding monumentally large marketing plans for their big films in a bid to create as much hype as possible and capture the attention of an audience now spoilt for choice. Then to earn the maximum impact from that hype, they flood the market at the time of a film's release, trying to monopolise the maximum number of theatrical screens on the opening weekend when curiosity about a film is at its peak. As more theatres go digital, it has become cheaper and logistically easier to release a film on more screens, since a print does not have to be physically delivered in such cases. The bigger the marketing blitzkrieg, the greater the audience anxiety to watch the film. In this fast-paced world of instant messaging that far outpaces instant coffee and 2 minute noodles, movie-goers no longer have the patience to wait for days, weeks or months to watch a high-profile film, as their parents and grandparents did. If it's being talked about in the press, it needs to be commented on at parties, and discussed on Facebook and Twitter. So almost everyone heads to theatres on the opening weekend.

An earlier generation of film marketers would worry about a handful of critics from the handful of media organisations in existence at the time. The media explosion of the past decade has translated into the advantage of *that* many more platforms on which to publicise your film, but also the double-edged sword of those many more spaces on which your film could be dismissed on its very opening day. Besides, in an era of FB, Twitter, BBM and blogs, every citizen is a potential critic who may choose to churn out opinions on a cellphone right there in the movie hall while watching the first day first show of a mammoth film. For films of this size that come accompanied by the huge hype their marketing teams generate, word of mouth travels at the speed of light in this age, and film companies need to guard against not just blatant piracy but also adverse public opinion sinking in and sinking their film. The logical thing to do then is to get as many human beings as possible into theatres before negative word of mouth or reviews have had an impact. If the audience and/or critical response have been positive, that can only serve to supplement your marketing tsunami. Then of course you know you will get the added bonus of longevity at theatres too.

The number of entertainment avenues vying for audience attention today is not the only reason for the scale at which film releases are now being planned. The other is the changing business model of corporates in the film business. Kamal Jain of Eros explains: 'Corporatisation through the emergence of the studio model has brought about a radical change in the functioning of the film industry. Studios like Eros have evolved a low-risk business model which involves pre-licensing a majority of a film's rights before its release. There has been a simultaneous increase in the number of avenues for monetisation of films. In addition to box-office revenues, we have cable and satellite rights, new media – Internet, VOD (video on demand), SVOD (subscription video on demand), DTH (direct to home), airlines and other platforms. So producers have to smartly plan windows for each stream to maximise the monetisation from each one of them. To put it simply, if you release the movie on satellite just as you release it in theatres, it will adversely affect theatrical collections. So you need to have a window for satellite, home video and every other platform. This is why the theatrical release has to be done in such a fashion as to earn the maximum revenue in two weeks, because by then another revenue stream is opening up to you. Besides, if as a corporate I have my own films coming to theatres every two weeks, I would like to maximise my revenue on a particular film in theatres before my next film comes along.'

In the past couple of years, this is the reason why we hear of film after film creating some opening weekend record or the other. Though film companies would prefer not to admit this on record, the truth is that a film's initial collections are not necessarily an indicator of its acceptance by the audience but a sign of the success of the marketing hype and/or faith in the reputation of the stars, director and production house.

This brings me back to my fixation in this book and that question we've left unanswered so far: are big films and poor marketing killing small films in Bollywood? Can something be done to prevent their death? Reliance Entertainment CEO Sanjeev Lamba admits that the industry is grappling with the challenge of how to market small, starless films and make them money spinners in their league. He adds: 'What we will hopefully see more of in future is an increase in the number of theatres across the country so that there are more screens available where big films can be released while leaving a sufficient number of screens free for small films too. But not every small film will look at this traditional route of a theatrical release to be followed by DVDs and satellite. Many will come directly to our homes and find success there.'

So it's possible that there will be a happily ever after for everyone involved. A lot is changing in the Mumbai film industry today. Big films are getting bigger and small films continue to struggle for recognition, though perhaps they're in a better position now than ever before... As mainstream Bollywood desperately seeks out ways to handle an increasingly restless and impatient audience, as big-star-driven films strive to overshadow everyone and everything else on the viewers' list of entertainment options, heroes – who are perceived as bigger crowd pullers than heroines – take home pay packets that are getting more generous by the day. Mindsets are marginally (but only marginally) changing with the super success of the Vidya Balan-centric *The Dirty Picture* in 2011 which ended up as one of the top 10 grossers of the year and Vidya's *Kahaani* in 2012. On a smaller scale, the box-office success of Imtiaz Ali's *Jab We Met* (2007) widely seen as a Kareena Kapoor-focused film, Madhur Bhandarkar's *Fashion* (2008) starring Priyanka Chopra and *No One Killed Jessica* (2011) with Rani Mukerji and Vidya have set the industry thinking that if they use greater imagination in writing and marketing, it's possible to create blockbusters with female characters as the focal point. Says Siddharth Roy Kapur, CEO, UTV Motion Pictures: 'This business of assuming that women-centric films are risky is a self-perpetuating myth. Because of this assumption, the industry does not invest in expensive films where women are the central characters and we don't market such films at the same scale as male-centric projects. Then when they don't make as much money as films with our leading men, we say, "Look, we were right, women-centric films don't work at the box office"'.

I remember conducting an interview with Madhuri Dixit years back where she'd lamented the fact that the industry tends to write strong female characters only in '*rona-dhona* [weepy] films' on social issues. 'There's nothing wrong with such films,' she clarified, 'but why don't we have more women too playing the main role in massy, *masala* films which are comedies? It's not like our lives are only about issues!'

Madhuri got that in her 1994 film *Hum Aapke Hain Koun!* which remains one of Hindi filmdom's highest grossers of all time till date. In the absence of a steady flow of such films, actresses are unable to build up larger-than-life images of the same magnitude as their male counterparts. In the absence of such an image, it's impossible to have crazed fan followings to match the men. Sans such followings, their films do not rake in initial collections equivalent to what heroes bring into theatres. Since that does not happen, the occasional heroine-centric film tends not to make as much money as the male-centric films flooding the market. And so we are back to square one: the industry considers such projects risky though they themselves are responsible for the situation.

If your glass is half full rather than half empty though, you will agree that some things are changing for the better. And at the forefront of this change is Vidya Balan. The world was a different place for Vidya when I first interviewed her in 2008. I was shooting one of the earliest episodes for my TV interview show at the time, and I remember being keen on getting her as a guest because I have always enjoyed watching her on screen. In those days, her acting seemed to be the last thing on the minds of most sections of the public, the press and even some of her industry colleagues, one of whom refused to do a joint interview with her on two occasions for my show. Back then, her girth and dress sense were the subject of much acerbic discussion, the paltry two years by which she is senior to Shahid Kapoor had been the target of acid attacks in the run-up to the release of their film *Kismat Konnection*, and it seemed like she could do nothing right! Worse, Vidya had stubbornly dug her heels in and decided that she would not watch either her weight or her wardrobe.

The tide began to turn with *Paa* the following year, when the country received a gentle reminder of the actress within the star. With *Ishqiya,* audiences and critics alike sat up and took notice of the sex appeal oozing out of every pore of this refreshingly un-skinny woman with a personality and physicality so distinct from her contemporaries. By then she had also lost some kilos and got herself more suitable fashion advice.

Today it seems Vidya Balan can do no wrong! The Vidya I interview for my book is far removed from the beleaguered star of 2008 – commercially successful without depending on major male stars as crutches, a National Award winner, darling of the media and the masses, a star who now appears to inspire a certain confidence in audiences that has so far been Aamir Khan's preserve…a conviction that if she's in a film, then there must be something special to it. And in an inexplicable twist of fate, the very qualities for which she was once slammed have become her USPs: she is now arguably a national brand ambassador for both the sari and the full-bodied Indian woman.

Her renewed self-confidence was evident throughout this interview which took place at the end of a gruelling day when she'd just finished dozens of Q&As to promote her latest film. Here are excerpts from our conversation that occurred almost – as our former Prime Minister may have noted – at the stroke of the midnight hour:

Me: Many people feel that the success of *The Dirty Picture* and *Kahaani* are an indicator that attitudes towards women are changing within the industry. But then there are some who feel it's a one-off occurrence. What's your take on this?

Vidya: Cinema is a reflection of reality. It mirrors what is happening in the world around us. The world over, women are firmly establishing themselves in hitherto uncharted territories, they are assuming centre stage. That the reins of a woman's life are in her own hands is therefore a realisation that's slowly but surely emerging. And that is what you're seeing in films today. We're therefore being seen as individuals with opinions, dreams, hopes, ambitions, aspirations, etc., of our own. We know that we have the right to make our own choices, we have the courage to stand up for ourselves, we have the power to avenge wrongs, etc.

That's what you see in films like *No One Killed Jessica* or *The Dirty Picture*. And that's why they've worked commercially. Even in a *Kahaani* where she could well have been a woman who is in a sorry state because she's pregnant and her husband has gone missing, you feel empathy for her but she's not someone you feel sorry for. And even if you feel sorry for her, you don't see her as a victim because she's being strong and she knows that she's going to fight to the very end to unravel the truth. There were such films made (with female protagonists) in the 1980s too but they rarely did well commercially probably because the story lines or the treatment spelt or voiced a need for change, a change that didn't seem imminent but seemed distant and hence not real or engaging.

Today's films work because they depict the changing world of a woman or change already underway which is always hopeful, inspiring and at the same time entertaining. And since we're humanising women in Hindi cinema, they've become more interesting. It's no longer an 'either or' situation. There's no judgement and therefore it's not glorification versus vilification. So you could use your sexuality to get ahead in life, you could be a mother and could well have desires of your own, you could be a widow and have an affair. The line between good and bad is anyway blurring in our cinema and we're dabbling more with the grey in our women characters. And really, it's a no-holds-barred situation for us. I myself have had the good fortune of portraying strong individuals in almost every film of mine. It's just that the expression, the situations or the circumstances have been different in film after film. So you get to see different avatars of today's woman, the modern Indian woman! I think that's what these films are a reflection of, so it's not a one-off occurrence. It's here to stay!!

However, not every film with a woman as central protagonist will work, simply because a female central protagonist isn't a *formula* for success. Having said that, a *good* film with a female central protagonist could work so what determines whether a film does well or not is whether or not it's a good film. Period!

Me: You say the reins of a woman's life are in her own hands, yet there is so much that is wrong with the position of women in our society today. Just look at the rate of female foeticide and infanticide in India, the attitude towards rape victims, the discrimination that women continue to face socially and professionally in both urban and rural areas, among the rich and the poor, among uneducated and supposedly educated sections of society…

Vidya: But change is a continuum. It is relative and never an absolute. We have come a long way but there's a longer way to go, and cinema only bears testimony to that evolution.

Me: What you're saying is similar to something Madhuri Dixit had said to me in an interview at the start of this decade. Obviously she was talking about the era in which she was working at the time. She said the problem with women-centric Hindi films is that they don't make fun, crazy, *masala* comedies with women…it's always meaningful cinema, and while there's nothing wrong with meaningful cinema, it's almost as though our lives are only about issues.

Vidya: While those 'meaningful' films will always get made, that situation isn't completely true any more. These days the most important cause is the self *(laughs)* and we are interesting and fun and crazy.

Me: Do you think though that we are a long way away from the day when let's say Shah Rukh and Aamir or a Salman, I mean a male star that big, would do a supporting role in a film which is woman-centric like *The Dirty Picture?*

Vidya: Yes, that probably won't happen for a while.

Me: Why is that?

Vidya: Because change doesn't happen overnight. These kind of films are just about beginning to get made, they're beginning to get accepted, they're beginning to do well. It's not going to change the status quo overnight. But I think it will happen at some point. Having said that, it's also fair, because I'm very clear about the fact that I don't want to do a role which is not exciting enough just because it's a big film, so I don't know why you would expect a male star to do a role in a woman-centric film, if it's not the greatest of roles.

Me: But I am talking about a strong supporting role like, let's say, Priyanka Chopra in *Kaminey*. She wasn't a central character but she was somebody who you came away remembering and respecting. I mean that kind of role.

Vidya: Okay, that kind of role.

Me: Major heroines in our industry do that all the time. It doesn't affect their brand. So when will the really major guys start doing that?

Vidya: It will happen…in time...I hope.

Me: Our film marketing seems to have become restricted to appearing on reality shows, holding a series of press conferences, giving a bunch of interviews. Are we being imaginative enough with our marketing?

Vidya: I think it's getting there. Film marketing is dynamic so every film dictates its own strategy. When I came in with *Parineeta* seven years ago, marketing was not really the done thing. A few interviews and city visits was all that we did. Even now we're using the more traditional methods but people are slowly pushing the envelope. Studios like UTV, Viacom 18, etc., have strong marketing teams. These are the guys who are bringing about that change. And I do see a lot of interesting ideas being thrown around. Okay, not lots, but it's happening. We still do dabble a lot in the traditional means because Anna, as a people, I think we're not the sort who just throw out a well-oiled machine. It takes us time to replace things. You know that the traditional methods work, so we're using that. But I do see interesting ideas once in a while.

Me: For instance?

Vidya: Hmm, okay now I'm a bit… Name the films?

Me: *Kahaani, The Dirty Picture, No One Killed Jessica, Ishqiya…*

Vidya: *Kahaani,* actually. The way the missing-person posters were put all over the city, it was not direct. It took people a while to realise that it's not really about a missing person, it's Arnab Bagchi's character in *Kahaani.*

Me: I want to ask you a question I had asked about *No One Killed Jessica*'s marketing to Siddharth Roy Kapur of UTV. I wondered if it was appropriate that you went on the show *Bigg Boss* to promote that film. Of course it's a high-TRP show, but this was a sensitively made film about a sensitive issue whereas *Bigg Boss* is not high-grade entertainment. Not that I have anything against reality shows, but it's a show that people might watch and yet not respect. So was it an appropriate platform for this film, or was it that every UTV film's team goes on *Bigg Boss,* everybody else from every other production house does too, so…?

Vidya: All the more reason why *No One Killed Jessica* needed a *Bigg Boss.* We were trying to make this film accessible to the lowest common denominator and *Bigg Boss* is a show that is watched. Rani and I went on the show but we were not trivialising the issue. I think that was a good platform. This was a film with a difference, and we wanted to make sure that people were well aware of it, that people would reach theatres. I would say that probably the more conventional films don't need it.

Me: How does one draw a line when it comes to film marketing? While promoting *Kahaani*, you made appearances as a pregnant woman. That definitely got you attention, but there are also some people who felt that maybe it's a little over the top. How do you react to that?

Vidya: I don't worry about that. I was not being disrespectful or insensitive towards anyone. I play a character who is pregnant in *Kahaani*. It's a mystery film where there was only so much I could talk about. So I thought this was the right way to draw attention to the film. You know it is about a pregnant woman who is on the look out for her missing husband, so I held the poster in my hand and I went around distributing pamphlets and it worked very well for us in terms of grabbing eyeballs. But tomorrow if I am playing a person who is probably physically challenged, I'm not going to use that to promote my film. It was apparent that there was no disrespect meant in the promotions of *Kahaani*.

Me: During the course of this exercise I conducted for this book over the past year, I've come across former Miss Indias and Mr Indias and others working in films they're not particularly comfortable with because they're struggling to get good films. For instance, Miss India World 2008 Parvathy Omanakuttan who I saw in this really really awful…I mean I'm not mincing words about it, but it was a very poor quality production and I remember meeting her a few years back and she had told me about how tough it is to get into the industry. There are some top models I've seen acting in films that you wouldn't even watch, films that are not on anybody's radar. You haven't been through similar situations but if a newcomer were to come to you for advice and say, 'Look Vidya, I've not been getting films and there's this offer I've got for a film which I know is crass, the script doesn't make sense, I'm not sure the film will be of great quality but does it hurt me to do this film? Will it spoil things for me or should I look at it as at least being an on-sets experience?' what would you say?

Vidya: If you know it's a production that you will not enjoy then you shouldn't do it. What kind of experience will you get from a cringe-worthy production or performance or character? I believe there are no rules! Everyone told me that if you've done television, the entry into films will be very difficult. But where there is a will, there is a way. However, you have to have the patience and have the faith in yourself to be able to hold it out. I do realise that people come from all parts of the country to this industry, and often they have to compromise because it's a matter of survival. But if it isn't that, and you can wait it out, you should. Even if you have to take up other jobs while you wait for the right opportunity as an actor, it's fine. But do what you believe in. Even if it is a half-minute role or one that you feel will get you attention or give you satisfaction as an actor, then do it.

Me: But if a person is completely unknown, can doing an awful film spoil a brand value when that brand value doesn't exist in the first place?

Vidya: I'm not saying don't do it because of what people will see. People only see talent, I assure you. I was extremely awkward in (the teleserial) *Hum Paanch*. If I had seen myself in

Hum Paanch, I don't know if I would have given myself work. But the fact is that I kept at it. I wanted to be an actor and I continued to do ads and I was learning along the way. I believed in whatever I was doing and I went ahead and did it. Don't do it because you have to, do it because you want to. So it's not about brand value. Even if people see 10 bad films of yours, if they see one good ad film and they spot the talent, you will get work. Don't be worried. At that stage, it's not as easy, but nothing is the beginning or the end of the world. That's very important to remember. Nothing can damage you permanently.

Me: The other change that seems to be happening in the industry is in the attitude towards an actress' age and marital status. Aishwarya Rai Bachchan has had a kid but people haven't just assumed that this means the end of the road for her. A considerable number of our heroines right now are touching 30 or are in their 30s. There has been a dramatic change from the time when you did *Kismat Konnection* and there was a lot you had to deal with because Shahid Kapoor happens to be a couple of years younger than you. When Bipasha Basu did *Bachna Ae Haseeno* with Ranbir Kapoor too there was nonsense spoken about her, but it was a little less when she did *Aa Dekhen Zara* with Neil Nitin Mukesh the following year. With *Ek Main Aur Ekk Tu* just three years later (in 2012), there's hardly been any gossip about the fact that Kareena Kapoor is a couple of years older than Imran Khan. What has changed?

Vidya: Anyway people are having relationships across age groups. There are young girls with really old men, there are older women with younger men. So it really doesn't matter. And gone are the days when people said you can't desire another person's wife. Our moral codes and norms have changed over time. So if you are desirable, whether you are married or not doesn't matter. That's the change. Similarly, after you become a mother, nothing's really changing because if you maintain yourself well for example, and I'm not just talking about the body, just if you maintain yourself well, don't let yourself go all over the place, if you are still interested in yourself, people will be interested in you.

Lastly and importantly, the other change that's taken place is that female lead roles are not only for teenagers. So there's more scope for actresses at different ages and stages of their lives. There are more roles being written for *women* finally. And once you grow from being a girl into being a woman, you are a woman forever so the possibilities are exciting.

There is truth in Vidya's words, but it's equally true that when a woman-centric Hindi film fares well at the box office, it's almost as though sections of the industry and society are looking for excuses for its success. When I review *The Dirty Picture* on my blog, a reader tweets me: 'What's the big deal? You might celebrate the fact that a film resting on the female lead's shoulders has become a hit, but let's face it, it's because Vidya showed her body that the film did well.'

Not fair, I write back, the ones who flash most flesh in the Hindi film industry these days happen to be men. Salman Khan is no longer the sole champion of shirtlessness among Bollywood's heroes. Every guy worth his biceps is stripping for the camera; male directors are happy to pander to the boys' envious male fans and unapologetically gawking female fans;

and the industry's few women directors too are not bashful about the female gaze. Director Zoya Akhtar had a shirtless Hrithik Roshan almost 'preening like a peacock' (as a friend of mine put it) in 2011's runaway hit *Zindagi Na Milegi Dobara*. Before Zoya, there was Farah Khan in 2007, making Shah Rukh Khan's 'six pack' a national talking point in her directorial venture *Om Shanti Om*. In the same year, for his debut film *Saawariya* released on the very same day, young Ranbir Kapoor dropped his towel to show off a tushy that the Censor Board decided Indians should not see. The following year, the Board was less stiff necked about John Abraham rising out of the ocean Ursula Andress-style wearing the briefest of golden briefs, or John scratching his bottom as he sleepily wandered around his apartment in only his underwear in *Dostana*. When Ranveer Singh took the audience's breath away with his cracker of a debut in *Band Baaja Baaraat* (2010), you would not have guessed that he had a body-baring bone in him. Yet there he was in his second film in December 2011 – *Ladies vs Ricky Bahl* – lazily stretching himself as he stood on a Goan beach in just his shorts, while the camera drank in every line and angle of that marvellously muscled body over which he must have laboured for hours at a gym.

This penchant for male toplessness has reached such heights in Bollywood that our heroes have even learnt to laugh at its compulsoriness and at themselves. In *Vicky Donor* (2012) which marks John's debut as a producer, he makes just one appearance...in a song accompanying the end credits. At one point while the music is still playing, he stops dancing for no particular reason and stands with arms open wide, offering himself up to the women around him who gently divest him of his jacket and hose him. It's almost as if this scene is as essential to the film as breathing is to life; as if he is saying to his audience, I know you want it, you know you want it, so let's forget about relevance to the plot. Is there a viewer out there who will cite such scenes to take away credit from Salman, Hrithik, Shah Rukh, Ranbir, Ranveer or John for the success of their films? So why is such treatment reserved for female stars? Is it fair to trivialise Vidya's success with *The Dirty Picture,* especially when it's obvious that her role required her to wear skimpy clothes? The reader to whom I shoot these questions responds with silence. So I throw them at another self-made woman in Bollywood, Vidya's contemporary Priyanka Chopra.

Me: Is there a tendency to look for excuses when women-centric films do well. There are those who'd like to believe that *The Dirty Picture* was successful only because Vidya showed skin. It's almost as though some people are watching and waiting for female-centric films to not do well. In your case, for instance, they'll easily forget *Fashion* but they'll remember that *Saat Khoon Maaf* didn't make money at the box office.

Priyanka: But whenever there is a change, the Indian mentality is to look for reasons for its downfall or success. We as a people, me included, are scared of change because we have had centuries of things being the way they are. We are used to letting things be. Change makes us insecure. We are used to films being run by male leads. We are used to men getting at least five times more screen space than women. If a hero signs up with a heroine, it suddenly makes her career really big. If a film stars a certain male so and so it will be sold at a higher price than if it stars the most successful heroine in Bollywood. But these things are changing. Today you will have a film being sold at a much bigger price than it probably would have five years ago if a Vidya Balan, Katrina Kaif, Kareena or I are in it, you know, females with certain credibility. It is a slow change. You cannot expect people to suddenly say, oh it's a female film so of course it will do well. It's a change to see a female promoting a film, it's new, it scares us *ki* oh my god will it change how we are used to seeing cinema?

Me: But are Hindi film heroes supportive enough of heroines? In Hollywood, guys as big as Pierce Brosnan and Colin Firth were willing to act in a film like *Mamma Mia* revolving around Meryl Streep. Why don't we find a Shah Rukh, Salman or Aamir willing to do the role that Arjan Bajwa played in *Fashion*?

Priyanka: That's the way our society is. We should be aware of that and not be delusional. We can't compare the way male and female actors are seen in Hollywood and Bollywood. Heroes run our film industry. It is changing to a certain extent, and I'm sure we will reach a point where female-centric movies will have actors who might just do a supporting part because of a relationship with the director or because they want to be supportive, but it doesn't happen right now and I don't think we should be holding up a gun and asking the actor, why don't you do it? Because that has been the norm for the longest time.

Me: In *Don 2* you had a small but significant role. In *Kaminey* there was no question that Shahid was the lead but you had a very significant supporting role. Do you think *Agneepath* gave you your due?

Priyanka: Okay, so I have a question. When you watched 3 *Idiots,* what did you feel about Kareena Kapoor's role in the film?

Me: That it was a small but significant supporting role...

Priyanka: ...It doesn't take away from the fact that she was an integral part of the film. Second of all, Madhavi's role in the old *Agneepath* was nothing compared to the role I have in my *Agneepath*. The film is about Vijay Deenanath Chauhan who is seeking revenge for his father's death. That is the essence of the film. I'm not going to be a part of it and say, oh my role needs to be a lot more. Because the essence of the film cannot be changed. Whether it was Rishi Kapoor's role or mine or Sanju sir's role, all of us centred around Hrithik's character Vijay. If there was more of my part, you would certainly watch the film and say, this romantic story is dragging, taking away from the essence of the story which is Vijay's revenge. So it is important for the film to be true to its one-line plot. How every other character supports that is important. I've never done films for the fact that I'll have the most important role. I do films because I like stories. *Agneepath* was a story I loved and I like being part of amazing films. I would do *Agneepath* all over again in a heartbeat if I had to, because it's a film I'm proud of being a part of.

Me: This really goes back to the earlier question, because we do know that no major male star in the industry would agree to do it if roles were reversed. I would not ask you the same question about *Kaminey* or even *Don 2,* but I do ask you about *Agneepath*... Won't a role of that length affect your brand value?

Priyanka: Not at all. Being a part of a film which is successful, and successful the way *Agneepath* has been, is a lot more important. See, box office is king, Anna. We can't deny that. Thankfully most directors come up to me and tell me, you know we have written this part for you, we have written this film for you, you're the only one who can do it. And I feel grateful because I didn't have a godfather in this industry, I didn't have anybody pushing me into films or making films for me. Today I have reached this status on my own and I take a lot of pride in that. Doing such a successful film, a film with an amazing story that I believe in, a director who I believed in from the time he narrated the story to me, doing such a film can't take away from brand value. On the contrary it would add to it because that many more people see you and love you even in the small part that you did.

I may dispute this point with Priyanka, but one thing we completely agree upon... The scene *is* changing in baby steps for Hindi film heroines. Be that as it may, it does seem like some other things will never change in this industry... Mumbai will continue to be the city of dreams; the Vipinnos and Vivek Sudershans of the world will continue to find their way to tinseltown; and some unfortunate journalist somewhere will continue to be traumatised by the experience of watching films like *Tum Hi To Ho*, *Impatient Vivek* and *Tension Doooor*.

10

'They Say I Look Like Dharmendra, Act Like Dilip Kumar!'

And...at...last...this...exercise...is...drawing...to...a... close...Forgive...me...for...the...Barbara...Cartland-style... punctuation...but...I'm...tired...to...the...point...of... delirium. This has been a great learning experience, without a doubt...but I admit that I have neither the energy, nor the money and time to go through this drill for another year. If you can understand what it means to both love and hate someone – or something – then you will appreciate the dichotomy of my feelings in this paragraph filled with joy that this assignment is ending and regret for precisely the same reason.

I wish you had been with me when I watched *Tension Doooor*. That unparalleled film-viewing experience would have brought home to you the genuine pleasure that accompanies the torture of watching the year's worst film. Masochism! I did say the word right at the start, didn't I?

I'm in Noida once again, that Uttar Pradesh suburb of Delhi which has become a second home to me in the past year. But today is not like every other visit here. It's my brother's birthday today so what the hell am I doing in the midst of all these necking couples in a multiplex, watching *Tension Doooor* with its four 'o's?! My soul brother Salman Khan said it right when he drawled: '*Ek baar jo maine* commitment *kar di, uske baad toh main khud ki bhi nahin sunta.*' (Once I have made a commitment, I don't listen to even myself.)

Tension Doooor is the story of Gopal (played by a gawky, stocky gentleman called Swaraaj Singh) who is involved in an accident that bestows on him the other-worldly ability to read people's thoughts. This, as you can imagine, causes great discomfort to the dishonest folk around him, in particular the village *mukhiya, pandit, ojha* and *vaid* – the headman, the priest, the exorcist and the medicine man – since Gopal tries to warn the unsuspecting village people about these unscrupulous men. As with the hero of Henrik Ibsen's *An Enemy of the People,* the crooks in this village manage to turn everyone against Gopal. I realise this is a wholly inappropriate and completely blasphemous reference considering the disparity in quality between Ibsen's play and *Tension Doooor,* but humour me please. As that old hymn goes, 'I am tired, I am weak, I am worn' and I'm prone to a few idiosyncrasies in this frame of mind!

As a child when I watched KL Saigal's *Devdas,* I was informed that the film was a classic but I remained highly amused by the exaggerated style of acting. Then when I saw old black-and-white films starring Sohrab Modi, I had a rollicking time as those junior artistes playing courtiers rolled their eyes and froze to indicate that they were shocked at the king's words. Never again! Never again will I look at a work of art without a context, without trying to understand a film's position within the time and space it occupies.

The poorly shot, poorly framed, poorly lit, poorly acted, poorly written *Tension Doooor* in 2011 is filled with extras who stiffen up and pop their eyeballs out at the camera, and scenes where groups of people speak in a chorus. In one song, the camera coyly travels from the lead couple to the surrounding flora and fauna before returning to the love birds prancing around on a stretch of green. How could a film manage to be so outmoded? And how could a director possibly descend to such depths? I discover from the Goddess Google and a conversation with the film's hero Swaraaj Singh that *Tension Doooor*'s director, the late Ambrish Singhal, was the man who directed the 1990s Kamal Sadanah-Ritu Shivpuri-starrer *Hum Sab Chor Hain*. You remember right – it's the film featuring that memorable Kumar Sanu number, 'Saawali saloni teri jheel si aankhen'. How do such things happen? How? How? How?

And how do I describe my Q&A with Swaraaj (parts of which I'm quoting in this chapter, unedited)? Ah yes, there's a euphemism for it. Interesting.

First that pressing question: Why are there four 'o's in the '*doooor*' of *Tension Doooor*? Much thought was apparently invested in the decision. '*Door*' with two 'o's could have been mistaken for the English word for the entrance to a room or building. Three 'o's were considered numerologically inauspicious. Hence '*doooor*'!

Swaraaj informs me that he has been involved in theatre for 15 years, since his days in Assam, home to his originally Haryanvi/Punjabi family. He now continues to devote time to that passion in Mumbai, juggling it with his family's gems and jewellery business.

I hold my peace when he describes *Tension Doooor* as a 'very nice, very entertaining film', adding, 'and those who have seen the film have liked it very much.'

I can understand this man's desire to act in this film that marks his feature debut, but it defies logic that *Tension Dooor*'s heroine Swati Anand is the very actress who plays Manjusha in the hit Zee TV soap *Pavitra Rishta*. Seriously! Why would a Bollywood aspirant who has a good thing going outside this industry, debase herself and risk her acting career on this decrepit film?! It's impossible to imagine that *Tension Doooor* could have seemed remotely attractive even on paper.

As these thoughts flash through my mind, Swaraaj gravely continues, 'This is not the first time I'm facing the camera. I've done some documentaries in Assam. So I enjoyed working on *Tension Doooor*. I've played Oedipus on stage. It's the greatest tragedy in the world. It happened in Greece in 1500 BC (not true, but never mind that). In India only two persons have played the role of Oedipus on stage – me and Naseeruddin Shah. All stage actors have a dream that one day they will play Oedipus. Some sort of natural calamity or natural disaster is involved with this play because it's about a person who killed his father, married his mother and produced children. Because it is against the natural thing, so whoever attempt this play they cannot succeed because of the things associated with it, so only very few people can succeed in doing this play. I am one of them.'

Swaraaj has a full-fledged career coming up on the big screen. I learn from him that he will play the lead in a forthcoming film called *Sorry Papa* which is about the relationship between a father and his mentally challenged daughter. And he gets to step into the role of Oedipus in a film. Oedipus might get a complex on hearing this disturbing news, though stranger things have been known to happen along the margins of Bollywood!

Having sampled Swaraaj's acting in *Tension Doooor*, I find that something about this information awakens a dormant devilish streak in me.

And so I ask straight-faced: How would you assess yourself as an actor? How good do you think you are? 'I am good actor,' he replies blithely. 'People in the film industry compliment me. In the press conference, Raza Murad (who actually acted in *Tension Doooor*!!!) has complimented that Swaraaj Singh is new Dharmendra in the film. And apart from that, I do the emotional role very more ease, and so people find the combination of Mr Dilip Kumar and Dharmendra in me, combination of tragedy and action, okay. They say so, first time there is combination of tragedy and action on the silver screen.'

By now I am struggling to maintain my composure. I quietly wonder what frame of mind actor Raza Murad was in when (and if) he delivered such commendations on a public platform. I ask: Dilip Kumar's acting and Dharmendra's looks,

did you say? Is Mr Murad the only one to have showered such praise on you or have others said so too? 'Others have, yes many people say that you look like Dharmendra many times, sometimes Rajendra Kumar the chocolate...'

I see.

Since I'm now at a loss for words, that seems as good a line as any on which to sign off.

Appendix I
Film Index

Here are details of the 121 films I watched and reviewed on my blog as part of my research for this book. Not all of them fall within the category of 'Bollywood' films as defined in the 'Author's Note' at the start of this book.

A

Aagaah The Warning
Director: Karan Razdan
Cast: Karan Razdan, Rituparna Sengupta, Satish Kaushik, Ila Arun, Atul Kulkarni, Anang Desai, Zakir Hussain, Anupam Kher
Language: Hindi

Aarakshan
Director: Prakash Jha
Cast: Amitabh Bachchan, Deepika Padukone, Manoj Bajpai, Saif Ali Khan, Prateik, Tanvi Azmi, Guest appearance by Hema Malini
Language: Hindi

Aashiqui.in
Director: Shankhadeep
Cast: Ankita Srivastava, Ishaan Manhaas
Language: Hindi

Always Kabhi Kabhi
Director: Roshan Abbas
Cast: Ali Fazal, Zoa Morani, Satyajeet Dubey, Giselli Monteiro, Navneet Nishan, Lillette Dubey
Language: Hindi with English
(Produced by Shah Rukh Khan's Red Chillies Entertainment)

Angel
Director: Ganesh Acharya
Cast: Maddalsa Sharma, Nilesh Sahay, Guest appearance by Sukhwinder Singh
Language: Hindi

***Ashoka The Hero* (animation)**
Director: Gaurav Jain
Cast: *The names of the voice cast were not listed on the film's official website. I received no response to my e-mails for details.*
Language: Hindi

Azaan
Director: Prashant Chadha
Cast: Sachiin J Joshi, Candice Boucher, Aarya Babbar, Dalip Tahil, Alyy Khan, Ravi Kissen, Vijayendra Ghatge, Sarita Choudhury
Language: Hindi and occasional dialogues in various other languages

B

Bas Ek Tamanna
Director: Rahul B. Kapoor
Cast: Reema Lagoo, Samir Aftab, Rituparna Sengupta, Gauri Karnik, SM Zaheer, Anjana Mumtaz, Vrijesh Hirjee, Master Laeeque
Language: Hindi

Bbuddah... Hoga Terra Baap
Director: Puri Jagannadh
Cast: Amitabh Bachchan, Sonu Sood, Prakash Raj, Hema Malini, Raveena Tandon, Sonal Chauhan, Charmme, Makrand Deshpande
Language: Hindi

Be-Careful
Director: Chandrakant Singh
Cast: Rajniesh Duggall, Zaid Hamid, Tanisha Mukherjee, Rajpal Yadav, Sanjay Mishra, Johnny Lever, Asrani, Tiku Talsania, Shakti Kapoor
Language: Hindi

Bheja Fry 2
Director: Sagar Ballary
Cast: Vinay Pathak, Kay Kay Menon, Minissha Lamba, Suresh Menon, Amole Gupte, Aditi Govitrikar
Language: Hindi

Bhindi Baazaar Inc
Director: Ankush Bhatt
Cast: Prashant Narayanan, Gautam Sharma, Pavan Malhotra, Piyush Mishra, Shilpa Shukla, Deepti Naval, Kay Kay Menon, Jackie Shroff
Language: Hindi

Bin Bulaye Baaraati
Director: Chandrakant Singh
Cast: Om Puri, Aftab Shivdasani, Priyanka Kothari, Sanjay Mishra, Rajpal Yadav, Vijay Raaz, Johnny Lever, Rati Agnihotri, Gulshan Grover, Guest appearances by Shweta Tiwari and Mallika Sherawat
Language: Hindi

Bodyguard
Director: Siddique

Cast: Salman Khan, Kareena Kapoor, Raj Babbar, Rajat Rawail, Vidya Sinha, Guest appearance by Katrina Kaif
Language: Hindi

Bubble Gum
Director: Sanjivan Lal
Cast: Delzad Sanjay Hiwale, Sohail Lakhani, Tanvi Azmi, Sachin Khedekar, Apoorva Arora, Suraj Singh
Language: Hindi

C

Chala Mussaddi Office Office
Director: Rajiv Mehra
Cast: Pankaj Kapoor, Gaurav Kapur, Manoj Pahwa, Sanjay Mishra, Deven Bhojani, Hemant Pandey, Asawari Joshi, Mahesh Thakur, Makrand Deshpande
Language: Hindi

Chalo Dilli
Director: Shashant Shah
Cast: Lara Dutta, Vinay Pathak, Rahul Singh, Guest appearances by Yana Gupta and Akshay Kumar
Language: Hindi
(Former Miss Universe Lara Dutta made her debut as a producer with this film)

Chargesheet
Director: Dev Anand
Cast: Dev Anand, Naseeruddin Shah, Milind Gunaji, Divya Dutta, Jackie Shroff, Aryan Vaid, Devshi Khanduri
Language: Hindi

Chatur Singh Two Star
Director: Ajay Chandhok
Cast: Sanjay Dutt, Ameesha Patel, Suresh Menon, Anupam Kher, Gulshan Grover, Satish Kaushik
Language: Hindi

Chillar Party
Director: Nitesh Tiwari, Vikas Bahl
Cast: Irrfan Khan, Sanath Menon, Rohan Grover, Naman Jain, Aarav Khanna, Vishesh Tiwari, Chinmai Chandranshuh, Vedant Desai, Shriya Sharma, Divij Handa, Guest appearance by Ranbir Kapoor
Language: Hindi
(Salman Khan was the film's co-producer)

Chitkabrey – Shades of Grey
Director: Suneet Arora
Cast: Ravi Kissen, Rahul Singh, Bobby Vats, Akshay Singh, Puja Gupta
Language: Hindi

Cycle Kick
Director: Shashi Sudigala
Cast: K.P. Nishan Nanaiah, Sunny Hinduja, Girija Oak, Ishita Sharma, Dwij Yadav, Tom Alter
Language: Hindi

D

Damadamm
Director: Swapna Waghmare Joshi
Cast: Himesh Reshammiya, Purbi Joshi, Sonal Sehgal
Language: Hindi

Dam 999

Director: Sohan Roy

Cast: Vinay Rai, Vimala Raman, Joshua Fredric Smith, Megha Burman, Linda Arsenio, Jaala Pickering, Ashish Vidyarthi, Rajit Kapoor, Jineet Rath

Language: English with occasional Malayalam dialogues

Delhi Belly

Director: Abhinay Deo

Cast: Imran Khan, Kunaal Roy Kapur, Vir Das, Poorna Jagannathan, Vijay Raaz, Shenaz Treasury, Rahul Singh

Language: English with some Hindi dialogues. A Hindi dubbed version of the film was released simultaneously.

(Co-produced by Aamir Khan)

Desi Boyz

Director: Rohit Dhawan

Cast: Akshay Kumar, John Abraham, Deepika Padukone, Chitrangda Singh, Anupam Kher, Bharti Achrekar, Sanjay Dutt

Language: Hindi

Dhobi Ghat (Mumbai Diaries)

Director: Kiran Rao

Cast: Prateik, Monica Dogra, Kriti Malhotra, Aamir Khan

Language: English and Hindi

Dil Toh Baccha Hai Ji

Director: Madhur Bhandarkar

Cast: Ajay Devgn, Emraan Hashmi, Omi Vaidya, Shazahn Padamsee, Tisca Chopra, Shruti Haasan, Shraddha Das, Rituparna Sengupta

Language: Hindi

The Dirty Picture
Director: Milan Luthria
Cast: Vidya Balan, Naseeruddin Shah, Emraan Hashmi, Tusshar Kapoor, Rajesh Sharma
Language: Hindi

***Don 2* (3D)**
Director: Farhan Akhtar
Cast: Shah Rukh Khan, Priyanka Chopra, Boman Irani, Kunal Kapoor, Alyy Khan, Lara Dutta, Om Puri, Nawwab Shah, Guest appearance by Hrithik Roshan
Language: Hindi

Double Dhamaal
Director: Indra Kumar
Cast: Sanjay Dutt, Arshad Warsi, Riteish Deshmukh, Jaaved Jaafery, Ashish Chowdhry, Mallika Sherawat, Kangna Ranaut, Satish Kaushik
Language: Hindi

Dum Maaro Dum
Director: Rohan Sippy
Cast: Abhishek Bachchan, Rana Daggubati, Bipasha Basu, Aditya Pancholi, Prateik Babbar, Guest appearance by Deepika Padukone
Language: Hindi

F

F.A.L.T.U.
Director: Remo D'souza
Cast: Jackky Bhagnani, Chandan Roy Sanyal, Angad Bedi, Puja Gupta, Riteish Deshmukh, Arshad Warsi, Vijay Kashyap, Rameshwari, Akbar Khan, Mahesh Thakur, Darshan Jariwala
Language: Hindi

Force

Director: Nishikant Kamat

Cast: John Abraham, Genelia D'souza, Vidyut Jamwal, Mohnish Bahl, Sandhya Mridul, Raj Babbar

Language: Hindi

404 Error Not Found

Director: Prawal Raman

Cast: Rajvvir Aroraa, Nishikant Kamat, Imaad Shah, Tisca Chopra, Satish Kaushik

Language: Hindi

G

Game

Director: Abhinay Deo

Cast: Abhishek Bachchan, Jimmy Sheirgill, Boman Irani, Shahana Goswami, Anupam Kher, Kangna Ranaut, Sarah-Jane Dias

Language: Hindi

Gandhi to Hitler

Director: Rakesh Ranjan Kumar

Cast: Raghuvir Yadav, Neha Dhupia, Avijit Dutt, Aman Verma, Nalin Singh

Language: Hindi

H

Happy Husbands

Director: Anay

Cast: Anay, Mohit Ghai, Kurush Deboo

Language: Hindi

Haunted **(3D)**
Director: Vikram Bhatt
Cast: Mahakshay, Tia Bajpai, Arif Zakaria, Achint Kaur, Mohan Kapoor
Language: Hindi

Hawai Dada
Director: Ajay Kartik
Cast: Anupam Kher, Gargi Datar, Tanuja, Tinnu Anand, Guest appearance by Vidya Balan
Language: Hindi

Hostel
Director: Manish Gupta
Cast: Vatsal Sheth, Tulip Joshi, Mukesh Tiwari
Language: Hindi

Hum Tum Shabana
Director: Sagar Ballary
Cast: Shreyas Talpade, Tusshar Kapoor, Minissha Lamba, Pia Trivedi, Satish Kaushik, Sanjay Mishra
Language: Hindi

I

I Am
Director: Onir
Cast: Nandita Das, Juhi Chawla, Manisha Koirala, Sanjay Suri, Rahul Bose, Purab Kohli, Anurag Kashyap, Radhika Apte, Abhimanyu Singh, Arjun Mathur
Language: Hindi, English, Kashmiri with a bit of Bengali, Kannada, Marathi

I Am Kalam

Director: Nila Madhab Panda

Cast: Harsh Mayar, Husaan Saad, Gulshan Grover, Pitobash, Beatrice Ordeix

Language: Hindi

I Am Singh

Director: Puneet Issar

Cast: Gulzar Inder Chahal, Tulip Joshi, Puneet Issar, Brooke Johnston

Language: Hindi with Punjabi and English

Impatient Vivek

Director: Rahat Kazmi

Cast: Vivek Sudershan, Sayali Bhagat, Hrishikesh Joshi, Charu Asopa

Language: Hindi

J

Jo Dooba So Paar, It's Love in Bihar

Director: Praveen Kumar

Cast: Anand Tiwari, Sita Ragione Spada, Vinay Pathak, Rajat Kapoor, Pitobash

Language: Hindi

Jo Hum Chahein

Director: Pawan Gill

Cast: Sunny Gill, Simran Mundi, Achint Kaur, Alyy Khan

Language: Hindi

K

Kaccha Limboo

Director: Sagar Ballary

Cast: Taher Sutterwala, Chinmay Kambli, Atul Kulkarni, Sarika, Guest appearances by Vinay Pathak and Rukhsar
Language: Hindi

Kashmakash
Director: Rituparno Ghosh
Cast: Raima Sen, Jisshu Sengupta, Riya Sen, Dhritiman Chatterjee, Prosenjit
Language: The original Bengali film *Noukadubi* was re-edited and dubbed in Hindi by producer Subhash Ghai and released as *Kashmakash* for north Indian audiences. Ghosh opted to stay away from the re-edit.

Khap
Director: Ajai Sinha
Cast: Uvika Choudhary, Sarrtaj Gill, Om Puri, Mohnish Bahl, Anuradha Patel, Manoj Pahwa, Govind Namdeo
Language: Hindi

Kucch Luv Jaisaa
Director: Barnali Ray Shukla
Cast: Shifaali Shah, Rahul Bose, Sumeet Raghvan, Guest appearances by Om Puri and Neetu Chandra
Language: Hindi

Kya Yahi Sach Hai
Director: YP Singh
Cast: Rajiv Roda, Bobby Vats
Language: Hindi
(Director YP Singh is a former IPS officer who based this film on his book Carnage by Angels *which is about corruption in the Indian civil services)*

L

Ladies vs Ricky Bahl

Director: Maneesh Sharma

Cast: Ranveer Singh, Anushka Sharma, Parineeti Chopra, Dipannita Sharma, Aditi Sharma

Language: Hindi

Lanka

Director: Maqbool Khan

Cast: Manoj Bajpayee, Arjan Bajwa, Tia Bajpai

Language: Hindi

Life Goes On

Director: Sangeeta Datta

Cast: Sharmila Tagore, Soha Ali Khan, Girish Karnad, Om Puri, Neerja Naik, Mukulika Banerjee

Language: English with Bengali

Loot

Director: Raj Thakur

Cast: Govinda, Suneil Shetty, Jaaved Jaaferi, Mahaakshay Chakraborty, Prem Chopra, Dalip Tahil, Ravi Kissen, Mahesh Manjrekar, Mika, Kim Sharma, Guest appearance by Rakhi Sawant

Language: Hindi

Love Breakups Zindagi

Director: Sahil Sangha

Cast: Diya Mirza, Zayed Khan, Cyrus Sahukar, Tisca Chopra, Farida Jalal, Satyadeep Mishra, Guest appearance by Shah Rukh Khan

Language: Hindi

Love Express

Director: Sunny Bhambhani

Cast: Sahil Mehta, Mannat Ravi, Vikas Katyal, Priyam Galav, Om Puri
Language: Hindi

Love You…Mr Kalakaar
Director: S Manasvi
Cast: Amrita Rao, Tusshar Kapoor, Ram Kapoor, Prem Chopra, Madhoo, Kiran Kumar, Yatin Karyekar
Language: Hindi

Luv ka the End
Director: Bumpy
Cast: Shraddha Kapoor, Taaha Shah
Language: Hinglish

M

Masti Express
Director: Vikram Pradhan
Cast: Rajpal Yadav, Divya Datta, Johnny Lever, Guest appearances by Shankar Mahadevan and Kashmira Shah
Language: Hindi

Mausam
Director: Pankaj Kapur
Cast: Shahid Kapoor, Sonam Kapoor, Anupam Kher, Supriya Pathak, Aditi Sharma
Language: Hindi

Memories In March
Director: Sanjoy Nag
Cast: Deepti Naval, Rituparno Ghosh, Raima Sen
Language: English, Hindi and a bit of Bengali

Men Will Be Men
Director: Gorky
Cast: Gaurav Chopraa, Rahil Tandon, Rajesh Kumar, Rohit Khurana, Zeenal Kamdar, Special appearance by Rajesh Khattar
Language: Hindi
(Produced by Red Chillies Idiot Box, the TV wing of Shah Rukh Khan's Red Chillies Entertainment)

Mere Brother ki Dulhan
Director: Ali Abbas Zafar
Cast: Katrina Kaif, Imran Khan, Ali Zafar, Kanwaljeet Singh, Parikshit Sahni, Tara D'Souza
Language: Hindi

Miley Naa Miley Hum
Director: Tanveer Khan
Cast: Chirag Paswan, Poonam Dhillon, Kabir Bedi, Kangna Ranaut, Sagarika Ghatge, Neeru Bajwa, Guest appearance by Shweta Tiwari
Language: Hindi

Mod
Director: Nagesh Kukunoor
Cast: Ayesha Takia Azmi, Rannvijay Singh Singha, Raghuvir Yadav, Tanve Azmi, Anant Mahadevan
Language: Hindi

Monica
Director: Sushen Bhatnagar
Cast: Divya Dutta, Ashutosh Rana, Rajit Kapoor, Kitu Gidwani
Language: Hindi

Mujhse Fraaandship Karoge
Director: Nupur Asthana

Cast: Saqib Saleem, Saba Azad, Nishant Dahiya, Tara D'Souza, Mita Vashisht
Language: Hindi

Mumbai Mast Kallander
Director: Aman Mihani
Cast: Mohsin Akhtar, Muzzi, Shilpa Shukla, Luna Lahkar
Language: Hindi

Mummy Punjabi
Director: Pammi Somal
Cast: Kirron Kher, Kanwaljeet Singh, Jackie Shroff, Sachin Sharma, Viraf Patel, Nimisha Goswami, Urvashi Gandhi, Simran Vaid, Guest appearance by Gurdass Mann
Language: English. A dubbed Hindi version was released simultaneously.

Murder 2
Director: Mohit Suri
Cast: Emraan Hashmi, Prashant Narayanan, Jacqueline Fernandez, Sudhanshu Pandey
Language: Hindi

My Friend Pinto
Director: Raaghav Dar
Cast: Prateik Babbar, Arjun Mathur, Shruti Seth, Kalki Koechlin, Makrand Deshpande, Divya Dutta
Language: Hindi
(Co-produced by Sanjay Leela Bhansali)

N

Na Jaane Kabse
Director: Pammi Somal

Cast: Garry Gill, Amrita Prakash, Sharat Sena, Lillette Dubey, Ayub Khan, Gurpreet Ghuggi, Himani Shivpi, Anju Mahendroo
Language: Hindi

Naughty @ 40
Director: Jag Mundhra
Cast: Govinda, Yuvika Chaudhary, Anupam Kher, Sanjay Mishra, Rakesh Bedi, Harish, Shakti Kapoor, Sayali Bhgat
Language: Hindi

No One Killed Jessica
Director: Raj Kumar Gupta
Cast: Rani Mukerji, Vidya Balan, Rajesh Shama, Neil Bhoopalam, Satyadeep Mishra, Bubbles Sabharwal, Samara Chopra, Myra Karn
Language: Hindi with some English

Not A Love Story
Director: Ram Gopal Varma
Cast: Mahie Gill, Deepak Dobriyal, Ajay Gehi, Zakir Hussain
Language: Hindi

P

Pappu Can't Dance Saala
Director: Saurabh Shukla
Cast: Neha Dhupia, Vinay Pathak, Rajat Kapoor, Guest appearance by Naseeruddin Shah
Language: Hindi

Patiala House
Director: Nikhil Advani
Cast: Akshay Kumar, Rishi Kapoor, Anushka Sharma, Hard Kaur, Dimple Kapadia, Guest appearances by several real-life cricketers including Nasser Hussain, Andrew Symonds, Sanjay Manjrekar and Nikhil Chopra
Language: Hindi

Phhir
Director: Girish Dhmija
Cast: Rajniesh Duggall, Adah Sharma, Roshni Chopra, Mohan Agashe
Language: Hindi

Pyaar ka Punchnama
Director: Luv Ranjan
Cast: Raayo, Divyenu, Kartik, Nushrat, Sonalli, Ishita
Language: Hindi

R

Ragini MMS
Director: Pavan Kirpalani
Cast: Raj Kumar Yadav, Kainaz Motivala
Language: Hindi

***Ra.One* (3D)**
Director: Anubhav Sinha
Cast: Shah Rukh Khan (in a double role), Kareena Kapoor, Armaan Verma, Arjun Rampal, Shahana Goswami, Tom Wu, Guest appearances by Priyanka Chopra, Sanjay Dutt and Rajinikanth
Language: Hindi
(Produced by Shah Rukh Khan's Red Chillies Entertainment)

Rascals
Director: David Dhawan
Cast: Ajay Devgn, Sanjay Dutt, Kangna Ranaut, Arjun Rampal
Language: Hindi

Ready
Director: Anees Bazmee
Cast: Salman Khan, Asin Thottumkal, Paresh Rawal, Mahesh

Manjrekar, Anuradha Patel, Mohan Joshi, Akhilendra Mishra, Sharat Saxena, Arya Babbar, Guest appearances by Sanjay Dutt, Ajay Devgn, Kangna Ranaut, Arbaaz Khan and Zarine Khan
Language: Hindi

Rivaaz
Director: Ashok Kumar Nanda
Cast: Ritisha Vijayvargiya, Manoj Biddvai, Deepti Naval, Vijay Raaz, Meghna Naidu, Shadika Randhawa, Alok Nath, Rajendra Gupta, Sayajee Shinde, Reema Lagoo, Guest appearance by Sambhavna Seth
Language: Hindi

Rockstar
Director: Imtiaz Ali
Cast: Ranbir Kapoor, Nargis Fakhri, Aditi Rao Hydari, Shernaz Patel, Shammi Kapoor, Piyush Mishra, Kumud Mishra
Language: Hindi

S

Saat Khoon Maaf
Director: Vishal Bhardwaj
Cast: Priyanka Chopra, Neil Nitin Mukesh, John Abraham, Irrfan Khan, Aleksandr Dyachenko, Annu Kapoor, Naseeruddin Shah, Usha Uthup, Vivaan Shah, Konkona Sensharma, Ruskin Bond
Language: Hindi

Saheb Biwi aur Gangster
Director: Tigmanshu Dhulia
Cast: Mahie Gill, Jimmy Sheirgill, Randeep Hooda, Rajeev Gupta, Vipin Sharma, Deepraj Rana, Shreya Narayan
Language: Hindi

Sahi Dhandhe Galat Bande
Director: Parvin Dabas
Cast: Parvin Dabas, Kuldip Ruhil, Vansh Bhardwaj, Ashish Nayyar, Sharat Saxena, Neena Kulkarni, Anupam Kher, Kiron Juneja Sippy, Yashpal Sharma, Tena Desae, Udit Khurana, Preeti Jhangiani
Language: Hindi
(Produced by Preeti Jhangiani)

Satrangee Parachute
Director: Vineet Khetrapal
Cast: Siddhartha Sanghani, Rajvi Patel, Sanjay Mishra, Jackie Shroff, Kay Kay Menon
Language: Hindi

Shagird
Director: Tigmanshu Dhulia
Cast: Nana Patekar, Mohit Ahlawat, Rimi Sen, Zakir Hussain, Anurag Kashyap
Language: Hindi

Shaitan
Director: Bejoy Nambiar
Cast: Kalki Koechlin, Neil Bhoopalam, Kirti Kulhari, Shiv Pandit, Gulshan Devaiya, Rajeev Khandelwal, Raj Kumar Yadav, Rajit Kapoor, Pavan Malhotra
Language: Hindi with English
(Co-produced by Anurag Kashyap)

Shakal Pe Mat Ja
Director: Shubh Mukherjee
Cast: Shubh Mukherjee, Aamna Sharif, Saurabh Shukla, Raghuvir Yadav, Chitrak Bandyopadhyay, Pratik Katare, Harsh Parekh
Language: Hindi
(Co-produced by actress Hrishitaa Bhatt)

Cast: Akshay Kumar, Sonam Kapoor, Bobby Deol, Irrfan Khan, Rimi Sen, Suneil Shetty, Celina Jaitley
Language: Hindi

That Girl In Yellow Boots
Director: Anurag Kashyap
Cast: Kalki Koechlin, Gulshan Devaiah, Prashant Prakash, Naseeruddin Shah, Puja Sarup, Kartik Krishnan, Guest appearance by Rajat Kapoor
Language: Hindi

Tum Hi To Ho
Director: Sanjay Goel
Cast: Vipinno, Madhavi Sharma, Jackie Shroff, Vivek Shauq
Language: Hindi

Turning 30
Director: Alankrita Shrivastava
Cast: Gul Panag, Tillotama Shome, Jeneva Talwar, Purab Kohli, Siddharth Makkar
Language: Mostly English, some Hindi
(Produced by Prakash Jha)

U

United Six
Director: Vishal Aryan Singh
Cast: Parvathy Omanakuttan, Luna Lahkar, Daisy Bopanna, Mahi, Isha Batwe, Pooja Sharma
Language: Hindi

Utt Pataang
Director: Srikant V. Velagaleti
Cast: Vinay Pathak, Mahie Gill, Mona Singh, Saurabh Shukla,

Sanjay Mishra, Delnaz Paul
Language: Hindi

V

Vikalp
Director: Sachin P Karande
Cast: Deepal Shaw, Nirmal Pandey
Language: Hindi

W

Who's There? Kaun Hai Wahan?
Director: Ejaz Ahmed
Cast: Rajbir, Kalpana Mathur, Gagan Kang
Language: Hindi

Y

Yamla Pagla Deewana
Director: Samir Karnik
Cast: Dharmendra, Sunny Deol, Bobby Deol, Kulraj Randhawa, Emma Brown Garrett, Nafisa Ali, Sucheta Khanna, Mukul Dev, Anupam Kher
Language: Hindi with Punjabi

Yeh Dooriyan
Director: Deepshikha Nagpal
Cast: Deepshikha Nagpal, Kaishav Arora, Kunika, Ayub Khan
Language: Hindi
(As the film's producer, director, leading lady, choreographer, story, screenplay and dialogues writer, executive producer and casting director, Deepshikha Nagpal earned a place in the Limca Book of Records *for having handled the maximum number of jobs for a single film.)*

Yeh Faasley
Director: Yogesh Mittal
Cast: Tena Desae, Anupam Kher, Pavan Malhotra, Rushad Rana, Suhasini Mulay, Seema Biswas
Language: Hindi

Yeh Saali Zindagi
Director: Sudhir Mishra
Cast: Irrfan Khan, Chitrangda Singh, Arunoday Singh, Aditi Rao Hydari, Sushant Singh, Yashpal Sharma, Prashant Narayanan
Language: Hindi

Ye Stupid Pyar
Director: Rakesh Jain
Cast: Jatin Khurana, Noopur, Akansha Shivhare
Language: Hindi

Z

Zindagi Na Milegi Dobara
Director: Zoya Akhtar
Cast: Hrithik Roshan, Farhan Akhtar, Abhay Deol, Katrina Kaif, Kalki Koechlin
Language: Hindi with English

Zokkomon
Director: Satyajit Bhatkal
Cast: Darsheel Safary, Anupam Kher (in a double role), Manjari Phadnis
Language: Hindi

Appendix II
Dr BK Tyagi's Concept Note For *Impatient Vivek* (Unedited)

Dear Anna Vetticad,
The concept was as follows:
DILLI DOORASTH or TIMIR (Darkness)

Concept
DILLI DOORASTH is an intense satirical thriller, throwing a spotlight at criminal culture and mentality of people and rawness in their thoughts. This film is based on theory of DARWIN "JISKI LAATHI USKI BAINSE" means that the one who is powerful, is the winner... and the greatest contradiction of this theory by Dr. Frances "That there is a language of GOD and there have been people like Mahatma Gandhi, Mother Teresa etc. who have always served for HUMANITY... the film is based on contradiction of both type of thoughts and confusions to understand the reality of life. The perspective of the concept is built around the latest development as art of human genome projects, that there is no junk genes, they may also have some function, which need to be yet researched.

Backdrop

Film sets in and around MEERUT area of Utter Pradesh which is merely 60-70 kms away from Delhi; the most developed place in India, but the differences in mentality and thoughts have a gap of a hundred years.

Characters

The strongest part of this film is the Characters; every character in the film portrays a part of the society and the system. How people are use to the corruption in the values, mentality and relations' but still they feel "they are right" .

Looks

All the characters would have special looks so we are quite particular about costumes and the looks of characters. Art work would also be an extremely important part of the film to create the backdrop as a character of story. The nice thing about this film is that it would portray an intense story, in an entertaining way. Especially the language of that area and its rugged look, which will add beauty to the film. Rustic locations and the total backdrop would be quite realistic and interesting; virginity in visuals and a depth in its content would be there...

Storyline:

Shruti is a beautiful and flamboyant girl studying in a college having dreams to become a journalist like her uncle who lives at Dilli with his son Annu and wife Deepti.... Shruti has a loving father, a superstitious mother and an arrogant brother Batosh in the family along with her childhood neighbor and so called friend Rani...

Here Pramod is a simple and sober boy; a MR by profession but surrounded with criminal bent of people all around. He has a friend

JAGGI who is an abductor by profession. Promod somehow goes to see Dr. Devender; father of Shruti for some professional reason and falls in love with Shruti, but at the same time he has a confrontation with Batosh....

It takes three months for him to chalk out a plan and he moves to Shruti's father, Dr. Devender, for seeking a help from him for the sale of his medicines. Promod takes the emotional edge from Dr. Devender when he tells him that he is from that village where Dr. Devender's sister has got married. Dr. Devender agrees to help him but the real motive of Promod is to see and to talk to Shruti.

Promod plan of getting close to Shruti succeeds and he starts luring the girl with the politeness and soft words of his. Shruti also reciprocates and Promod starts taking that Shruti has also fallen in love with him.

There, Batosh is carving the designs to retain his power of land holdings and in the meanwhile he has a sudden confrontation with Promod resulting to a scuffle between both.

The soft edge of the story continues and Promod comes to see Shruti's family for inviting them for the marriage ceremony of his sister. In the marriage ceremony, Promod gets chance to come closer to Shruti confirming his belief that Shruti has also fallen in love with him

Carried away with his own emotions and belief, Promod comes to Shruti's father with the intention of asking for the matrimonial alliance of his with Shruti but to the maximum grief and surprise, Shruti refuses for any feelings for him. Promod is heart-broken but he still takes that Shruti may have denied because of the fear of her parents. On the provocation by his accomplice, Jaggi Promod abducts

Shruti with the hope that he will be able to get his love while Shruti is away from the fear of her family.

The abduction of Shruti creates the rave among her family members and the cousin of Shruti, Annu who comes to the village to see the things of his own. Annu moves to the police but there is no response from the authorities. Annu is accompanied by a local politician named Sirohe ji. There Promod is subjected to severe emotional turmoil by Shruti who refuses his hand in marriage and dismisses for any feeling for him. Promod along with his family is now in soup. He has abducted the girl on belief that everything will be okay once both of them get married. But the refusal of the girl has totally changed the situation. Now if he leaves the girl, a statement of the girl would put his entire family behind the bars.

The police are after him. Now, Jaggi and others ask him to marry the girl forcibly, if he wants to save himself and his family. In this situation, the challenge before Shruti is to save herself from the wrath of Pramod and his family. She pretends before the Promod and his family as if she is possessed by the spirit of Pramod's grandmother. Now Pramod and his family start taking care of Shruti, believing the act of Shruti to be the will of Pramod grandmother's.

There police is hard-pressed by Annu's efforts and his father's political connections and speed up the investigation.

The speedy investigation by the police made Annu a hero in the eyes of everybody in the town. This was very frustrating for Batosh as he could not do anything for his sister but his cousin; Annu is now in the town and he is doing what Batosh could not do.

Batosh also has a fear that Annu may ask for his share in the land holdings.

The story moves here with thrilling twists to show the survival tactics adopted by Pramod and his family, and Shruti who is still in the custody of Pramod's family. She is trying to save herself by pretending to be possessed while the emotional lover Promod had got churned in the whole drama. He is not a criminal but the circumstances make him entangled in criminal activities. Promod's father asks Jaggi to eliminate Annu. On the other side Batosh is also carving designs to do so...

Suddenly somebody shoots at Annu. When this news comes to Promod, he believes that this is done by his father Rameshwar and so he repents and releases Shruti asking her to go back because he has by then become fed up of the problems and turmoil happening in his life just for getting her love.

Who shot at Annu and what happens to Promod after that? Why the struggle for survival makes people behave differently ---is the crux of the story.

hope it will serve your purpose........

Appendix III

A Contest For My Readers... And A Big Thank You

I began *annavetticadgoes2themovies* as an experiment. I had intended to derive a book from my blog right from the moment I started it, but I was not certain what form it would take. And I'm not sure I could have sustained the motivation for this book through an entire year of back-breaking research, if it weren't for the response I received to my blog from readers worldwide. As I wrapped up my manuscript, I felt it would be incomplete unless I actively involved them in these pages. You have already read some of them quoted in Chapter 5. And coming up below are winning entries for an informal contest I held on my blog, inviting readers to send me 200 word reviews of any 2011 Bollywood film that I had already reviewed. To repeat the point I made when I announced the contest, 'As Uriah Heep might have said... This is just my 'umble way of saying thank you to the social media and the blogosphere.'

Thank you to everyone who participated, and congratulations to winners Laya Maheshwari, Tanvi Agarwal, Kanisha Raina and Shrey Khetarpal. I hope you enjoy having your reviews reproduced here (unedited) as promised. A signed copy of the book is on its way to each of you.

FIRST PRIZE: LAYA MAHESHWARI

Zindagi Na Milegi Dobara

With *Zindagi Na Milegi Dobara,* Zoya Akhtar achieved the impossible. She made a film about the White People Problems meme without any actual Caucasians in the leads. On the surface, *Zindagi...* is a film that seems to be heart-warming and uplifting. But once you peek a little closer, you realise how facile its façade is. It must be easy to ruminate about how pointless materialistic pursuits are when said rumination is being done on a plush sofa inside a posh villa in a pretty Spanish locale with a powerful car parked outside, while clad in branded and – no doubt – expensive clothes. It must be easy to laugh at your friend throwing another friend's phone out of the window when you know the first friend has enough money to readily buy another phone. Ultimately, *Zindagi...* is a film made by people with money starring people with money portraying people with money with a message about how money isn't important in our lives.

Yeah, right.

Tell me that in a sequel set 5 years in the future which has Hrithik's character holidaying and enjoying life while paying the rent on his apartment now that he's quit his Wall Street job.

SECOND PRIZE: TANVI AGARWAL

Don 2

A suave, sexy antagonist not only dons the role of protagonist, but also charms and takes the audience on a fun ride. That's the power and pull of *Don 2,* and I'm not merely referring to SRK's magnetism.

The cast, cinematography and screenplay all contribute towards a polished entertainer.

Farhan Akhtar reasserts himself as a competent director by delivering a pulsatingly enjoyable and technically slick film. While *Don 2*'s story could be tighter and is less intricate than *Don 1*'s, Farhan succeeds in surprising the viewer as his clever twists unfold alongside Don's well-crafted heist. He employs Shankar-Ehsaan-Loy's music minimally yet effectively to propel his narrative, which comprises several adrenaline-pumping moments. A particular car chase and fist fight sequence deserve special mention. The vulnerable romance between SRK and Priyanka, whose palpable chemistry scorches the screen, also commands appreciation.

Any discourse on *Don 2* is incomplete without commenting on SRK's androgynous swagger, flamboyant sex appeal, and wickedly witty dialogues. SRK makes bad look really good, just as a swelteringly fit Priyanka makes hot look cool. As if that weren't enthusing enough, an ingenious flash of Don's license plate in the penultimate sequence only leaves the audience yearning for more.

THIRD PRIZE (TIE): KANISHA RAINA

The Dirty Picture

The words that define *The Dirty Picture* get sung over and over again in the film – '*arra ra nakka mukka*'. What is the movie if not a treat for your senses? Yes, it's loud, it's crass, it's dirty, but how could a film based on Silk Smitha or similar dancing femme fatales be any different or deserve any lesser treatment? The movie moves smoothly from a small village to the grand Madras film industry in very carefully edited scenes which are brightened up with powerful dialogues. What also works well for the movie are the strong supporting characters right from the mild-mannered Ramakant who has always lived in his brother's shadow to money-minded producer Selva Ganesh. Yet it's Vidya Balan's movie through and through. Her acting prowess, her seductive moves, her candour and screen presence take you by surprise. The film's music helps the character and the story grow and its treatment is classic '80s. The movie, however, loses steam towards the end which seems like a stretch after the very fluid first half. Silk deserved a larger-than-life end – as ironical as it may sound.

THIRD PRIZE (TIE): SHREY KHETARPAL

Pyaar ka Punchnama

Director Luv Ranjan's *Pyaar Ka Punchnama* is a film I didn't watch initially but got hold of a DVD based on at least 10 recommendations from my male friends. 'Incredibly sexist' and 'crude' are the words that first came to mind. However, I did find myself enjoying it for all its exaggerations, outrageous yet funny writing and the fine performances by the cast of newcomers. It is a film about three boys who are used, abused and treated like dogs by the girls in their lives.

There are no stereotypes that the makers left out in showcasing the 'cold-hearted' women in the film: the nagging girlfriend; the 'loose' working woman who wears short skirts; the unpredictable pretty girl at work who gives out all the wrong signals but only wants to be friends!

PKP is the kind of film that PETA would make if they were working to protect men or the reverse of Ms Taslima Nasreen's tweets about men. There is also a long monologue about the cruelty of women by one of the guys in the film that went viral. *PKP* is an average comedy for a boys-only viewing and for girls who do not mind sexist jokes.